# 比较文学与世界文学 研究丛书

主编 曹顺庆

三编 第 **23** 册

出自一本书的 180 个成语（上）

吴 国 珍 编译

花木兰文化事业有限公司

国家图书馆出版品预行编目资料

出自一本书的 180 个成语（上）／吴国珍 编译 –– 初版 –– 新
北市：花木兰文化事业有限公司，2024〔民 113 〕
目 6+184 面；19×26 公分
（比较文学与世界文学研究丛书 三编 第 23 册）
ISBN 978-626-344-822-3（精装）
1.CST：论语 2.CST：成语 3.CST：注释 4.CST：白话译文
810.8                                                    113009377

ISBN-978-626-344-822-3

9 786263 448223

## 比较文学与世界文学研究丛书

三编　第二三册　　　　　　　　ISBN：978-626-344-822-3

## 出自一本书的 180 个成语（上）

编　　译 吴国珍
主　　编 曹顺庆
企　　划 四川大学双一流学科暨比较文学研究基地
总 编 辑 杜洁祥
副总编辑 杨嘉乐
编辑主任 许郁翎
编　　辑 潘玟静、蔡正宣　美术编辑 陈逸婷
出　　版 花木兰文化事业有限公司
发 行 人 高小娟
联络地址 台湾 235 新北市中和区中安街七二号十三楼
　　　　　电话：02-2923-1455／传真：02-2923-1452
网　　址 http://www.huamulan.tw 信箱 service@huamulans.com
印　　刷 普罗文化出版广告事业
初　　版 2024 年 9 月
定　　价 三编 26 册（精装）新台币 70,000 元　　版权所有 请勿翻印

# 出自一本书的180个成语(上)

吴国珍 编译

## 作者简介

吴国珍，男，1945 年出生于福建晋江。1969 年毕业于厦门大学外文系。从事英语教学 34 年。长期从事"四书"研究及英译。译作《论语最新英文全译全注本》于 2014 年由国家汉办推荐为孔子学院读物。主要著作:《论语最新英文全译全注本》《孟子最新英文全译全注本》《大学中庸最新英文全译全注本》(福建教育出版社) 等 5 本。《论语:平解英译》《孟子大学中庸:平解英译》(北京出版社) 2 本。《英汉唐诗朗诵》《庄子寓言故事》(巴黎友丰书店) 等 7 本。

## 提　　要

　　《论语》是中华优秀传统文化的重要源头活水。《论语》中的许多词语已经成为中文语言系统里面的成语，一直活跃在我们的文字系统和日常口语中。本书将这些成语汇集在一起，用中英文加以诠释并给出实际使用时的句例，对于普通读者的学习和应用定会大有裨益。

　　该书为收入的每个成语提供所在章节的原文，并有现代文今译和难字注释，且标明篇章，方便读者查阅原文以便深入学习。为了方便国外读者和国内英语爱好者，论语原文还配有英文翻译。

　　这些英文出自作者早期出版的《论语最新英文全译全注本》。该书于 2014 年成为全球孔子学院的推荐读物。正文英译的下面紧接着是一条英文解读，为国外读者解释该段原文的主旨或背景知识。

　　由于年代的变迁，书中的一些成语的意思已有变化。作者注意到这一点，故给每个成语配有两个英译。前一个用原意，第二个用新意。

　　该书的另一个亮点是配有中英文句例。限于篇幅，作者给每个成语仅提供两个句例，但已把每个成语可能出现的新旧用法都照顾到了。

　　作者为编纂此书查阅了大量的中英文资料，作过较长时间的分析研究，力求使成语的今译符合传统辞书的解读。我们希望广大读者能喜欢这本书，并因此而喜欢上中国的传统的文化。

# 比较文学的中国路径

曹顺庆

自德国作家歌德提出"世界文学"观念以来，比较文学已经走过近二百年。比较文学研究也历经欧洲阶段、美洲阶段而至亚洲阶段，并在每一阶段都形成了独具特色学科理论体系、研究方法、研究范围及研究对象。中国比较文学研究面对东西文明之间不断加深的交流和碰撞现况，立足中国之本，辩证吸纳四方之学，而有了如今欣欣向荣之景象，这套丛书可以说是应运而生。本丛书尝试以开放性、包容性分批出版中国比较文学学者研究成果，以观中国比较文学学术脉络、学术理念、学术话语、学术目标之概貌。

## 一、百年比较文学争讼之端——比较文学的定义

什么是比较文学？常识告诉我们：比较文学就是文学比较。然而当今中国比较文学教学实际情况却并非完全如此。长期以来，中国学术界对"什么是比较文学？"却一直说不清，道不明。这一最基本的问题，几乎成为学术界纠缠不清、莫衷一是的陷阱，存在着各种不同的看法。其中一些看法严重误导了广大学生！如果不辨析这些严重误导了广大学生的观点，是不负责任、问心有愧的。恰如《文心雕龙·序志》说"岂好辩哉，不得已也"，因此我不得不辩。

其中一个极为容易误导学生的说法，就是"比较文学不是文学比较"。目前，一些教科书郑重其事地指出：比较文学不是文学比较。认为把"比较"与"文学"联系在一起，很容易被人们理解为用比较的方法进行文学研究的意思。并进一步强调，比较文学并不等于文学比较，并非任何运用比较方法来进行的比较研究都是比较文学。这种误导学生的说法几乎成为一个定论，

一个基本常识，其实，这个看法是不完全准确的。

让我们来看看一些具体例证，请注意，我列举的例证，对事不对人，因而不提及具体的人名与书名，请大家理解。在 Y 教授主编的教材中，专门设有一节以"比较文学不是文学比较"为题的内容，其中指出"比较文学界面临的最大的困惑就是把'比较文学'误读为'文学比较'"，在高等院校进行比较文学课程教学时需要重点强调"比较文学不是文学比较"。W 教授主编的教材也称"比较文学不是文学的比较"，因为"不是所有用比较的方法来研究文学现象的都是比较文学"。L 教授在其所著教材专门谈到"比较文学不等于文学比较"，因为，"比较"已经远远超出了一般方法论的意义，而具有了跨国家与民族、跨学科的学科性质，认为将比较文学等同于文学比较是以偏概全的。"J 教授在其主编的教材中指出，"比较文学并不等于文学比较"，并以美国学派雷马克的比较文学定义为根据，论证比较文学的"比较"是有前提的，只有在地域观念上跨越打通国家的界限，在学科领域上跨越打通文学与其他学科的界限，进行的比较研究才是比较文学。在 W 教授主编的教材中，作者认为，"若把比较文学精神看作比较精神的话，就是犯了望文生义的错误，一百余年来，比较文学这个名称是名不副实的。"

从列举的以上教材我们可以看出，首先，它们在当下都仍然坚持"比较文学不是文学比较"这一并不完全符合整个比较文学学科发展事实的观点。如果认为一百余年来，比较文学这个名称是名不副实的，所有的比较文学都不是文学比较，那是大错特错！其次，值得注意的是，这些教材在相关叙述中各自的侧重点还并不相同，存在着不同程度、不同方面的分歧。这样一来，错误的观点下多样的谬误解释，加剧了学习者对比较文学学科性质的错误把握，使得学习者对比较文学的理解愈发困惑，十分不利于比较文学方法论的学习、也不利于比较文学学科的传承和发展。当今中国比较文学教材之所以普遍出现以上强作解释，不完全准确的教科书观点，根本原因还是没有仔细研究比较文学学科不同阶段之史实，甚至是根本不清楚比较文学不同阶段的学科史实的体现。

实际上，早期的比较文学"名"与"实"的确不相符合，这主要是指法国学派的学科理论，但是并不包括以后的美国学派及中国学派的学科理论，如果把所有阶段的学科理论一锅煮，是不妥当的。下面，我们就从比较文学学科发展的史实来论证这个问题。"比较文学不是文学比较""comparative literature is not literary comparison"，只是法国学派提出的比较文学口号，只是法国学派一派的主张，而不是整个比较文学学科的基本特征。我们不能够把这个阶段性的比较文学口号扩大化，甚至让其突破时空，用于描述比较文学所有的阶段和学派，更不能够使其"放之四海而皆准"。

法国学派提出"比较文学不是文学比较"，这个"比较"（comparison）是他们坚决反对的！为什么呢，因为他们要的不是文学"比较"（literary comparison），而是文学"关系"（literary relationship），具体而言，他们主张比较文学是实证的国际文学关系，是不同国家文学的影响关系，influences of different literatures，而不是文学比较。

法国学派为什么要反对"比较"（comparison），这与比较文学第一次危机密切相关。比较文学刚刚在欧洲兴起时，难免泥沙俱下，乱比的情形不断出现，暴露了多种隐患和弊端，于是，其合法性遭到了学者们的质疑：究竟比较文学的科学性何在？意大利著名美学大师克罗齐认为，"比较"（comparison）是各个学科都可以应用的方法，所以，"比较"不能成为独立学科的基石。学术界对于比较文学公然的质疑与挑战，引起了欧洲比较文学学者的震撼，到底比较文学如何"比较"才能够避免"乱比"？如何才是科学的比较？

难能可贵的是，法国学者对于比较文学学科的科学性进行了深刻的的反思和探索，并提出了具体的应对的方法：法国学派采取壮士断臂的方式，砍掉"比较"（comparison），提出比较文学不是文学比较（comparative literature is not literary comparison），或者说砍掉了没有影响关系的平行比较，总结出了只注重文学关系（literary relationship）的影响（influences）研究方法论。法国学派的创建者之一基亚指出，比较文学并不是比较。比较不过是一门名字没取好的学科所运用的一种方法……企图对它的性质下一个严格的定义可能是徒劳的。基亚认为：比较文学不是平行比较，而仅仅是文学关系史。以"文学关系"为比较文学研究的正宗。为什么法国学派要反对比较？或者说为什么法国学派要提出"比较文学不是文学比较"，因为法国学派认为"比较"（comparison）实际上是乱比的根源，或者说"比较"是没有可比性的。正如巴登斯佩哲指出："仅仅对两个不同的对象同时看上一眼就作比较，仅仅靠记忆和印象的拼凑，靠一些主观臆想把可能游移不定的东西扯在一起来找点类似点，这样的比较决不可能产生论证的明晰性"。所以必须抛弃"比较"。只承认基于科学的历史实证主义之上的文学影响关系研究（based on scientificity and positivism and literary influences.）。法国学派的代表学者卡雷指出：比较文学是实证性的关系研究："比较文学是文学史的一个分支：它研究拜伦与普希金、歌德与卡莱尔、瓦尔特·司各特与维尼之间，在属于一种以上文学背景的不同作品、不同构思以及不同作家的生平之间所曾存在过的跨国度的精神交往与实际联系。"正因为法国学者善于独辟蹊径，敢于提出"比较文学不是文学比较"，甚至完全抛弃比较（comparison），以防止"乱比"，才形成了一套建立在"科学"实证性为基础的、以影响关系为特征的"不比较"的比较文学学科理论体系，这终于挡住了克罗齐等人对比较文学"乱比"的批判，形成了以"科学"实证为特征的文学影响关系研究，确立了法国学派的学科理论和一整套方法论体系。当然，法国学派悍然砍掉比较研究，又不放弃"比较文学"这个名称，于是不可避免地出现了比较文学名不副实的尴尬现象，出现了打着比较文学名号，而又不比较的法国学派学科理论，这才是问题的关键。

当然，法国学派提出"比较文学不是文学比较"，只注重实证关系而不注重文学比较和文学审美，必然会引起比较文学的危机。这一危机终于由美国著名比较文学家韦勒克（René Wellek）在 1958 年国际比较文学协会第二次大会上明确揭示出来了。在这届年会上，韦勒克作了题为《比较文学的危机》的挑战性发言，对"不比较"的法国学派进行了猛烈批判，宣告了倡导平行比较和注重文学审美的比较文学美国学派的诞生。韦勒克作了题为《比较文学的危机》的挑战性发言，对当时一统天下的法国学派进行了猛烈批判，宣告了比较文学美国学派的诞生。韦勒克说："我认为，内容和方法之间的人为界线，渊源和影响的机械主义概念，以及尽管是十分慷慨的但仍属文化民族主义的动机，是比较文学研究中持久危机的症状。"韦勒克指出："比较也不能仅仅局限在历史上的事实联系中，正如最近语言学家的经验向文学研究者表明的那样，比较的价值既存在于事实联系的影响研究中，也存在于毫无历史关系的语言现象或类型的平等对比中。"很明显，韦勒克提出了比较文学就是要比较（comparison），就是要恢复巴登斯佩哲所讽刺和抛弃的"找点类似点"的平行比较研究。美国著名比较文学家雷马克（Henry Remak）在他的著名论文《比较文学的定义与功用》中深刻地分析了法国学派为什么放弃"比较"（comparison）的原因和本质。他分析说："法国比较文学否定'纯粹'的比较（comparison），它忠实于十九世纪实证主义学术研究的传统，即实证主义所坚持并热切期望的文学研究的'科学性'。按照这种观点，纯粹的类比不会得出任何结论，尤其是不能得出有更大意义的、系统的、概括性的结论。……既然值得尊重的科学必须致力于因果关系的探索，而比较文学必须具有科学性，因此，比较文学应该研究因果关系，即影响、交流、变更等。"雷马克进一步尖锐地指出，"比较文学"不是"影响文学"。只讲影响不要比较的"比较文学"，当然是名不副实的。显然，法国学派抛弃了"比较"（comparison），但是仍然带着一顶"比较文学"的帽子，才造成了比较文学"名"与"实"不相符合，造成比较文学不比较的尴尬，这才是问题的关键。

美国学派最大的贡献，是恢复了被法国学派所抛弃的比较文学应有的本义——"比较"（The American school went back to the original sense of comparative literature ——"comparison"），美国学派提出了标志其学派学科理论体系的平行比较和跨学科比较："比较文学是一国文学与另一国或多国文学的比较，是文学与人类其他表现领域的比较。"显然，自从美国学派倡导比较文学应当比较（comparison）以后，比较文学就不再有名与实不相符合的问题了，我们就不应当再继续笼统地说"比较文学不是文学比较"了，不应当再以"比较文学不是文学比较"来误导学生！更不可以说"一百余年来，比较文学这个名称是名不副实的。"不能够将雷马克的观点也强行解释为"比较文学不是比较"。因为在美国学派看来，比较文学就是要比较（comparison）。比较文学就是要恢复被巴登斯佩哲所讽刺和抛弃的"找点类似点"的平行比较研究。因为平行研究的可比性，正是类同性。正如韦勒克所说，"比较的价值既存在于事实联系的影响研究中，也存在于毫无历史关系的语言现象或类型的平等对比中。"恢复平行比较研究、跨学科研究，形成了以"找点类似点"的平行研究和跨学科研究为特征的比较文学美国学派学科理论和方法论体系。美国学派的学科理论以"类型学"、"比较诗学"、"跨学科比较"为主，并拓展原属于影响研究的"主题学"、"文类学"等领域，大大扩展比较文学研究领域。

## 二、比较文学的三个阶段

下面，我们从比较文学的三个学科理论阶段，进一步剖析比较文学不同阶段的学科理论特征。现代意义上的比较文学学科发展以"跨越"与"沟通"为目标，形成了类似"层叠"式、"涟漪"式的发展模式，经历了三个重要的学科理论阶段，即：

一、欧洲阶段，比较文学的成形期；二、美洲阶段，比较文学的转型期；三、亚洲阶段，比较文学的拓展期。我们将比较文学三个阶段的发展称之为"涟漪式"结构，实际上是揭示了比较文学学科理论的继承与创新的辩证关系：比较文学学科理论的发展，不是以新的理论否定和取代先前的理论，而是层叠式、累进式地形成"涟漪"式的包容性发展模式，逐步积累推进。比较文学学科理论发展呈现为层叠式、"涟漪"式、包容式的发展模式。我们把这个模式描绘如下：

法国学派主张比较文学是国际文学关系，是不同国家文学的影响关系。形成学科理论第一圈层：比较文学——影响研究；美国学派主张恢复平行比较，形成学科理论第二圈层：比较文学——影响研究＋平行研究＋跨学科研究；中国学派提出跨文明研究和变异研究，形成学科理论第三圈层：比较文学——影响研究＋平行研究＋跨学科研究＋跨文明研究＋变异研究。这三个圈层并不互相排斥和否定，而是继承和包容。我们将比较文学三个阶段的发展称之为层叠式、"涟漪"式、包容式结构，实际上是揭示了比较文学学科理论的继承与创新的辩证关系。

法国学派提出，可比性的第一个立足点是同源性，由关系构成的同源性。同源性主要是针对影响关系研究而言的。法国学派将同源性视作可比性的核心，认为影响研究的可比性是同源性。所谓同源性，指的是通过对不同国家、不同民族和不同语言的文学的文学关系研究，寻求一种有事实联系的同源关系，这种影响的同源关系可以通过直接、具体的材料得以证实。同源性往往建立在一条可追溯关系的三点一线的"影响路线"之上，这条路线由发送者、接受者和传递者三部分构成。如果没有相同的源流，也就不可能有影响关系，也就谈不上可比性，这就是"同源性"。以渊源学、流传学和媒介学作为研究的中心，依靠具体的事实材料在国别文学之间寻求主题、题材、文体、原型、思想渊源等方面的同源影响关系。注重事实性的关联和渊源性的影响，并采用严谨的实证方法，重视对史料的搜集和求证，具有重要的学术价值与学术意义，仍然具有广阔的研究前景。渊源学的例子：杨宪益，《西方十四行诗的渊源》。

比较文学学科理论的第二阶段在美洲，第二阶段是比较文学学科理论的转型期。从 20 世纪 60 年代以来，比较文学研究的主要阵地逐渐从法国转向美国，平行研究的可比性是什么？是类同性。类同性是指是没有文学影响关系的不同国家文学所表现出的相似和契合之处。以类同性为基本立足点的平行研究与影响研究一样都是超出国界的文学研究，但它不涉及影响关系研究的放送、流传、媒介等问题。平行研究强调不同国家的作家、作品、文学现象的类同比较，比较结果是总结出于文学作品的美学价值及文学发展具有规律性的东西。其比较必须具有可比性，这个可比性就是类同性。研究文学中类同的：风格、结构、内容、形式、流派、情节、技巧、手法、情调、形象、主题、文类、文学思潮、文学理论、文学规律。例如钱钟书《通感》认为，中国诗文有一种描写手法，古代批评家和修辞学家似乎都没有拈出。宋祁《玉楼春》词有句名句："红杏枝头春意闹。"这与西方的通感描写手法可以比较。

**比较文学的又一次危机：比较文学的死亡**

九十年代，欧美学者提出，比较文学作为一门学科已经死亡！最早是英国学者苏珊·巴斯奈特 1993 年她在《比较文学》一书中提出了比较文学的死亡论，认为比较文学作为一门学科，在某种意义上已经死亡。尔后，美国学者斯皮瓦克写了一部比较文学专著，书名就叫《一个学科的死亡》。为什么比较文学会死亡，斯皮瓦克的书中并没有明确回答！为什么西方学者会提出比较文学死亡论？全世界比较文学界都十分困惑。我们认为，20 世纪 90 年代以来，欧美比较文学继"理论热"之后，又出现了大规模的"文化转向"。脱离了比较文学的基本立场。首先是不比较，即不讲比较文学的可比性问题。西方比较文学研究充斥大量的 Culture Studies（文化研究），已经不考虑比较的合理性，不考虑比较文学的可比性问题。第二是不文学，即不关心文学问题。西方学者热衷于文化研究，关注的已经不是文学性，而是精神分析、政治、性别、阶级、结构等等。最根本的原因，是比较文学学科长期围于西方中心论，有意无意地回避东西方不同文明文学的比较问题，基本上忽略了学科理论的新生长点，比较文学学科理论缺乏创新，严重忽略了比较文学的差异性和变异性。

要克服比较文学的又一次危机，就必须打破西方中心论，克服比较文学学科理论一味求同的比较文学学科理论模式，提出适应当今全球化比较文学研究的新话语。中国学派，正是在此次危机中，提出了比较文学变异学研究，总结出了新的学科理论话语和一套新的方法论。

中国大陆第一部比较文学概论性著作是卢康华、孙景尧所著《比较文学导论》，该书指出："什么是比较文学？现在我们可以借用我国学者季羡林先生的解释来回答了:'顾名思义,比较文学就是把不同国家的文学拿出来比较,这可以说是狭义的比较文学。广义的比较文学是把文学同其他学科来比较,包括人文科学和社会科学'。"[1]这个定义可以说是美国雷马克定义的翻版。不过,该书又接着指出:"我们认为最精炼易记的还是我国学者钱钟书先生的说法:'比较文学作为一门专门学科,则专指跨越国界和语言界限的文学比较'。更具体地说,就是把不同国家不同语言的文学现象放在一起进行比较,研究他们在文艺理论、文学思潮,具体作家、作品之间的互相影响。"[2]这个定义似乎更接近法国学派的定义,没有强调平行比较与跨学科比较。紧接该书之后的教材是陈挺的《比较文学简编》,该书仍旧以"广义"与"狭义"来解释比较文学的定义,指出:"我们认为,通常说的比较文学是狭义的,即指超越国家、民族和语言界限的文学研究……广义的比较文学还可以包括文学与其他艺术(音乐、绘画等)与其他意识形态(历史、哲学、政治、宗教等)之间的相互关系的研究。"[3]中国比较文学早期对于比较文学的定义中凸显了很强的不确定性。

由乐黛云主编,高等教育出版社 1988 年的《中西比较文学教程》,则对比较文学定义有了较为深入的认识,该书在详细考查了中外不同的定义之后,该书指出:"比较文学不应受到语言、民族、国家、学科等限制,而要走向一种开放性,力图寻求世界文学发展的共同规律。"[4]"世界文学"概念的纳入极大拓宽了比较文学的内涵,为"跨文化"定义特征的提出做好了铺垫。

随着时间的推移,学界的认识逐步深化。1997 年,陈惇、孙景尧、谢天振主编的《比较文学》提出了自己的定义:"把比较文学看作跨民族、跨语言、跨文化、跨学科的文学研究,更符合比较文学的实质,更能反映现阶段人们对于比较文学的认识。"[5]2000 年北京师范大学出版社出版了《比较文学概论》修订本,提出:"什么是比较文学呢?比较文学是一种开放式的文学研究,它具有宏观的视野和国际的角度,以跨民族、跨语言、跨文化、跨学科界限的各种文学关系为研究对象,在理论和方法上,具有比较的自觉意识和兼容并包的特色。"[6]这是我们目前所看到的国内较有特色的一个定义。

---

1 卢康华、孙景尧著《比较文学导论》,黑龙江人民出版社 1984,第 15 页。

2 卢康华、孙景尧著《比较文学导论》,黑龙江人民出版社 1984 年版。

3 陈挺《比较文学简编》,华东师范大学出版社 1986 年版。

4 乐黛云主编《中西比较文学教程》,高等教育出版社 1988 年版。

5 陈惇、孙景尧、谢天振主编《比较文学》,高等教育出版社 1997 年版。

6 陈惇、刘象愚《比较文学概论》,北京师范大学出版社 2000 年版。

具有代表性的比较文学定义是 2002 年出版的杨乃乔主编的《比较文学概论》一书，该书的定义如下："比较文学是以跨民族、跨语言、跨文化与跨学科为比较视域而展开的研究，在学科的成立上以研究主体的比较视域为安身立命的本体，因此强调研究主体的定位，同时比较文学把学科的研究客体定位于民族文学之间与文学及其他学科之间的三种关系：材料事实关系、美学价值关系与学科交叉关系，并在开放与多元的文学研究中追寻体系化的汇通。"[7]方汉文则认为："比较文学作为文学研究的一个分支学科，它以理解不同文化体系和不同学科间的同一性和差异性的辩证思维为主导，对那些跨越了民族、语言、文化体系和学科界限的文学现象进行比较研究，以寻求人类文学发生和发展的相似性和规律性。"[8]由此而引申出的"跨文化"成为中国比较文学学者对于比较文学定义所做出的历史性贡献。

我在《比较文学教程》中对比较文学定义表述如下："比较文学是以世界性眼光和胸怀来从事不同国家、不同文明和不同学科之间的跨越式文学比较研究。它主要研究各种跨越中文学的同源性、变异性、类同性、异质性和互补性，以影响研究、变异研究、平行研究、跨学科研究、总体文学研究为基本方法论，其目的在于以世界性眼光来总结文学规律和文学特性，加强世界文学的相互了解与整合，推动世界文学的发展。"[9]在这一定义中，我再次重申"跨国""跨学科""跨文明"三大特征，以"变异性""异质性"突破东西文明之间的"第三堵墙"。

"首在审己，亦必知人"。中国比较文学学者在前人定义的不断论争中反观自身，立足中国经验、学术传统，以中国学者之言为比较文学的危机处境贡献学科转机之道。

## 三、两岸共建比较文学话语——比较文学中国学派

中国学者对于比较文学定义的不断明确也促成了"比较文学中国学派"的生发。得益于两岸几代学者的垦拓耕耘，这一议题成为近五十年来中国比较文学发展中竖起的最鲜明、最具争议性的一杆大旗，同时也是中国比较文学学科理论研究最有创新性，最亮丽的一道风景线。

---

7 杨乃乔主编《比较文学概论》，北京大学出版社 2002 年版。
8 方汉文《比较文学基本原理》，苏州大学出版社 2002 年版。
9 曹顺庆《比较文学教程》，高等教育出版社 2006 年版。

比较文学"中国学派"这一概念所蕴含的理论的自觉意识最早出现的时间大约是 20 世纪 70 年代。当时的台湾由于派出学生留洋学习，接触到大量的比较文学学术动态，率先掀起了中外文学比较的热潮。1971 年 7 月在台湾淡江大学召开的第一届"国际比较文学会议"上，朱立元、颜元叔、叶维廉、胡辉恒等学者在会议期间提出了比较文学的"中国学派"这一学术构想。同时，李达三、陈鹏翔（陈慧桦）、古添洪等致力于比较文学中国学派早期的理论催生。如 1976 年，古添洪、陈慧桦出版了台湾比较文学论文集《比较文学的垦拓在台湾》。编者在该书的序言中明确提出："我们不妨大胆宣言说，这援用西方文学理论与方法并加以考验、调整以用之于中国文学的研究，是比较文学中的中国派"[10]。这是关于比较文学中国学派较早的说明性文字，尽管其中提到的研究方法过于强调西方理论的普世性，而遭到美国和中国大陆比较文学学者的批评和否定；但这毕竟是第一次从定义和研究方法上对中国学派的本质进行了系统论述，具有开拓和启明的作用。后来，陈鹏翔又在台湾《中外文学》杂志上连续发表相关文章，对自己提出的观点作了进一步的阐释和补充。

在"中国学派"刚刚起步之际，美国学者李达三起到了启蒙、催生的作用。李达三于 60 年代来华在台湾任教，为中国比较文学培养了一批朝气蓬勃的生力军。1977 年 10 月，李达三在《中外文学》6 卷 5 期上发表了一篇宣言式的文章《比较文学中国学派》，宣告了比较文学的中国学派的建立，并认为比较文学中国学派旨在"与比较文学中早已定于一尊的西方思想模式分庭抗礼。由于这些观念是源自对中国文学及比较文学有兴趣的学者，我们就将含有这些观念的学者统称为比较文学的'中国'学派。"并指出中国学派的三个目标：1、在自己本国的文学中，无论是理论方面或实践方面，找出特具"民族性"的东西，加以发扬光大，以充实世界文学；2、推展非西方国家"地区性"的文学运动，同时认为西方文学仅是众多文学表达方式之一而已；3、做一个非西方国家的发言人，同时并不自诩能代表所有其他非西方的国家。李达三后来又撰文对比较文学研究状况进行了分析研究，积极推动中国学派的理论建设。[11]

继中国台湾学者垦拓之功，在 20 世纪 70 年代末复苏的大陆比较文学研

10 古添洪、陈慧桦《比较文学的垦拓在台湾》，台湾东大图书公司 1976 年版。
11 李达三《比较文学研究之新方向》，台湾联经事业出版公司 1978 年版。

究亦积极参与了"比较文学中国学派"的理论建设和学科建设。

季羡林先生 1982 年在《比较文学译文集》的序言中指出："以我们东方文学基础之雄厚，历史之悠久，我们中国文学在其中更占有独特的地位，只要我们肯努力学习，认真钻研，比较文学中国学派必然能建立起来，而且日益发扬光大"[12]。1983 年 6 月，在天津召开的新中国第一次比较文学学术会议上，朱维之先生作了题为《比较文学中国学派的回顾与展望》的报告，在报告中他旗帜鲜明地说："比较文学中国学派的形成（不是建立）已经有了长远的源流，前人已经做出了很多成绩，颇具特色，而且兼有法、美、苏学派的特点。因此，中国学派绝不是欧美学派的尾巴或补充"[13]。1984 年，卢康华、孙景尧在《比较文学导论》中对如何建立比较文学中国学派提出了自己的看法，认为应当以马克思主义作为自己的理论基础，以我国的优秀传统与民族特色为立足点与出发点，汲取古今中外一切有用的营养，去努力发展中国的比较文学研究。同年在《中国比较文学》创刊号上，朱维之、方重、唐弢、杨周翰等人认为中国的比较文学研究应该保持不同于西方的民族特点和独立风貌。1985 年，黄宝生发表《建立比较文学的中国学派：读〈中国比较文学〉创刊号》，认为《中国比较文学》创刊号上多篇讨论比较文学中国学派的论文标志着大陆对比较文学中国学派的探讨进入了实际操作阶段。[14]1988 年，远浩一提出"比较文学是跨文化的文学研究"（载《中国比较文学》1988 年第 3 期）。这是对比较文学中国学派在理论特征和方法论体系上的一次前瞻。同年，杨周翰先生发表题为"比较文学：界定'中国学派'，危机与前提"（载《中国比较文学通讯》1988 年第 2 期），认为东方文学之间的比较研究应当成为"中国学派"的特色。这不仅打破比较文学中的欧洲中心论，而且也是东方比较学者责无旁贷的任务。此外，国内少数民族文学的比较研究，也应该成为"中国学派"的一个组成部分。所以，杨先生认为比较文学中的大量问题和学派问题并不矛盾，相反有助于理论的讨论。1990 年，远浩一发表"关于'中国学派'"（载《中国比较文学》1990 年第 1 期），进一步推进了"中国学派"的研究。此后直到 20 世纪 90 年代末，中国学者就比较文学中国学派的建立、理论与方法以及相应的学科理论等诸多问题进行了积极而富有成效的探讨。

12 张隆溪《比较文学译文集》，北京大学出版社 1984 年版。
13 朱维之《比较文学论文集》，南开大学出版社 1984 年版。
14 参见《世界文学》1985 年第 5 期。

刘介民、远浩一、孙景尧、谢天振、陈淳、刘象愚、杜卫等人都对这些问题付出过不少努力。《暨南学报》1991 年第 3 期发表了一组笔谈，大家就这个问题提出了意见，认为必须打破比较文学研究中长期存在的法美研究模式，建立比较文学中国学派的任务已经迫在眉睫。王富仁在《学术月刊》1991 年第 4期上发表"论比较文学的中国学派问题"，论述中国学派兴起的必然性。而后，以谢天振等学者为代表的比较文学研究界展开了对"X+Y"模式的批判。比较文学在大陆复兴之后，一些研究者采取了"X+Y"式的比附研究的模式，在发现了"惊人的相似"之后便万事大吉，而不注意中西巨大的文化差异性，成为了浅度的比附性研究。这种情况的出现，不仅是中国学者对比较文学的理解上出了问题，也是由于法美学派研究理论中长期存在的研究模式的影响，一些学者并没有深思中国与西方文学背后巨大的文明差异性，因而形成"X+Y"的研究模式，这更促使一些学者思考比较文学中国学派的问题。

经过学者们的共同努力，比较文学中国学派一些初步的特征和方法论体系逐渐凸显出来。1995 年，我在《中国比较文学》第 1 期上发表《比较文学中国学派基本理论特征及其方法论体系初探》一文，对比较文学在中国复兴十余年来的发展成果作了总结，并在此基础上总结出中国学派的理论特征和方法论体系，对比较文学中国学派作了全方位的阐述。继该文之后，我又发表了《跨越第三堵'墙'创建比较文学中国学派理论体系》等系列论文，论述了以跨文化研究为核心的"中国学派"的基本理论特征及其方法论体系。这些学术论文发表之后在国内外比较文学界引起了较大的反响。台湾著名比较文学学者古添洪认为该文"体大思精，可谓已综合了台湾与大陆两地比较文学中国学派的策略与指归，实可作为'中国学派'在大陆再出发与实践的蓝图"[15]。

在我撰文提出比较文学中国学派的基本特征及方法论体系之后，关于中国学派的论争热潮日益高涨。反对者如前国际比较文学学会会长佛克马（Douwe Fokkema）1987 年在中国比较文学学会第二届学术讨论会上就从所谓的国际观点出发对比较文学中国学派的合法性提出了质疑，并坚定地反对建立比较文学中国学派。来自国际的观点并没有让中国学者失去建立比较文学中国学派的热忱。很快中国学者智量先生就在《文艺理论研究》1988 年第

---

15 古添洪《中国学派与台湾比较文学界的当前走向》，参见黄维梁编《中国比较文学理论的垦拓》167 页，北京大学出版社 1998 年版。

1 期上发表题为《比较文学在中国》一文，文中援引中国比较文学研究取得的成就，为中国学派辩护，认为中国比较文学研究成绩和特色显著，尤其在研究方法上足以与比较文学研究历史上的其他学派相提并论，建立中国学派只会是一个有益的举动。1991 年，孙景尧先生在《文学评论》第 2 期上发表《为"中国学派"一辩》，孙先生认为佛克马所谓的国际主义观点实质上是"欧洲中心主义"的观点，而"中国学派"的提出，正是为了清除东西方文学与比较文学学科史中形成的"欧洲中心主义"。在 1993 年美国印第安纳大学举行的全美比较文学会议上，李达三仍然坚定地认为建立中国学派是有益的。二十年之后，佛克马教授修正了自己的看法，在 2007 年 4 月的"跨文明对话——国际学术研讨会（成都）"上，佛克马教授公开表示欣赏建立比较文学中国学派的想法[16]。即使学派争议一派繁荣景象，但最终仍旧需要落点于学术创见与成果之上。

比较文学变异学便是中国学派的一个重要理论创获。2005 年，我正式在《比较文学学》[17]中提出比较文学变异学，提出比较文学研究应该从"求同"思维中走出来，从"变异"的角度出发，拓宽比较文学的研究。通过前述的法、美学派学科理论的梳理，我们也可以发现前期比较文学学科是缺乏"变异性"研究的。我便从建构中国比较文学学科理论话语体系入手，立足《周易》的"变异"思想，建构起"比较文学变异学"新话语，力图以中国学者的视角为全世界比较文学学科理论提供一个新视角、新方法和新理论。

比较文学变异学的提出根植于中国哲学的深层内涵，如《周易》之"易之三名"所构建的"变易、简易、不易"三位一体的思辨意蕴与意义生成系统。具体而言，"变易"乃四时更替、五行运转、气象畅通、生生不息；"不易"乃天上地下、君南臣北、纲举目张、尊卑有位；"简易"则是乾以易知、坤以简能、易则易知、简则易从。显然，在这个意义结构系统中，变易强调"变"，不易强调"不变"，简易强调变与不变之间的基本关联。万物有所变，有所不变，且变与不变之间存在简单易从之规律，这是一种思辨式的变异模式，这种变异思维的理论特征就是：天人合一、物我不分、对立转化、整体关联。这是中国古代哲学最重要的认识论，也是与西方哲学所不同的"变异"思想。

---

16 见《比较文学报》2007 年 5 月 30 日，总第 43 期。
17 曹顺庆《比较文学学》，四川大学出版社 2005 年版。

由哲学思想衍生于学科理论，比较文学变异学是"指对不同国家、不同文明的文学现象在影响交流中呈现出的变异状态的研究，以及对不同国家、不同文明的文学相互阐发中出现的变异状态的研究。通过研究文学现象在影响交流以及相互阐发中呈现的变异，探究比较文学变异的规律。"[18]变异学理论的重点在求"异"的可比性，研究范围包含跨国变异研究、跨语际变异研究、跨文化变异研究、跨文明变异研究、文学的他国化研究等方面。比较文学变异学所发现的文化创新规律、文学创新路径是基于中国所特有的术语、概念和言说体系之上探索出的"中国话语"，作为比较文学第三阶段中国学派的代表性理论已经受到了国际学界的广泛关注与高度评价，中国学术话语产生了世界性影响。

## 四、国际视野中的中国比较文学

文明之墙让中国比较文学学者所提出的标识性概念获得国际视野的接纳、理解、认同以及运用，经历了跨语言、跨文化、跨文明的多重关卡，国际视野下的中国比较文学书写亦经历了一个从"遍寻无迹""只言片语"而"专篇专论"，从最初的"话语乌托邦"至"阶段性贡献"的过程。

二十世纪六十年代以来港台学者致力于从课程教学、学术平台、人才培养，国内外学术合作等方面巩固比较文学这一新兴学科的建立基石，如淡江文理学院英文系开设的"比较文学"（1966），香港大学开设的"中西文学关系"（1966）等课程；台湾大学外文系主编出版之《中外文学》月刊、淡江大学出版之《淡江评论》季刊等比较文学研究专刊；后又有台湾比较文学学会（1973 年）、香港比较文学学会（1978）的成立。在这一系列的学术环境构建下，学者前贤以"中国学派"为中国比较文学话语核心在国际比较文学学科理论、方法论中持续探讨，率先启声。例如李达三在 1980 年香港举办的东西方比较文学学术研讨会成果中选取了七篇代表性文章，以 *Chinese-Western Comparative Literature: Theory and Strategy* 为题集结出版，[19]并在其结语中附上那篇"中国学派"宣言文章以申明中国比较文学建立之必要。

学科开山之际，艰难险阻之巨难以想象，但从国际学者相关言论中可见西方对于中国比较文学学科的发展抱有的希望渺小。厄尔·迈纳（Earl Miner）

---

18 曹顺庆主编《比较文学概论》，高等教育出版社 2015 年版。

19 *Chinese-Western Comparative Literature：Theory & Strategy*, Chinese Univ Pr.1980-6

在 1987 年发表的 *Some Theoretical and Methodological Topics for Comparative Literature* 一文中谈到当时西方的比较文学鲜有学者试图将非西方材料纳入西方的比较文学研究中。(until recently there has been little effort to incorporate non-Western evidence into Western com- parative study.) 1992 年，斯坦福大学教授 David Palumbo-Liu 直接以《话语的乌托邦：论中国比较文学的不可能性》为题（*The Utopias of Discourse: On the Impossibility of Chinese Comparative Literature*）直言中国比较文学本质上是一项"乌托邦"工程。(My main goal will be to show how and why the task of Chinese comparative literature, particularly of pre-modern literature, is essentially a *utopian* project.) 这些对于中国比较文学的诘难与质疑，今美国加州大学圣地亚哥分校文学系主任张英进教授在其 1998 编著的 *China in a polycentric world: essays in Chinese comparative literature* 前言中也不得不承认中国比较文学研究在国际学术界中仍然处于边缘地位（The fact is, however, that Chinese comparative literature remained marginal in academia, even though it has developed closely with the rest of literary studies in the United Stated and even though China has gained increasing importance in the geopolitical world order over the past decades.)。[20]但张英进教授也展望了下一个千年中国比较文学研究的蓝景。

新的千年新的气象，"世界文学""全球化"等概念的冲击下，让西方学者开始注意到东方，注意到中国。如普渡大学教授斯蒂文·托托西（Tötösy de Zepetnek, Steven）1999 年发长文 *From Comparative Literature Today Toward Comparative Cultural Studies* 阐明比较文学研究更应该注重文化的全球性、多元性、平等性而杜绝等级划分的参与。托托西教授注意到了在法德美所谓传统的比较文学研究重镇之外，例如中国、日本、巴西、阿根廷、墨西哥、西班牙、葡萄牙、意大利、希腊等地区，比较文学学科得到了出乎意料的发展（emerging and developing strongly）。在这篇文章中，托托西教授列举了世界各地比较文学研究成果的著作，其中中国地区便是北京大学乐黛云先生出版的代表作品。托托西教授精通多国语言，研究视野也常具跨越性，新世纪以来也致力于以跨越性的视野关注世界各地比较文学研究的动向。[21]

---

20 Moran T . Yingjin Zhang, Ed. China in a Polycentric World: Essays in Chinese Comparative Literature[J].现代中文文学学报,2000,4(1):161-165.

21 Tötösy de Zepetnek, Steven. "From Comparative Literature Today Toward Comparative Cultural Studies." CLCWeb: Comparative Literature and Culture 1.3 (1999):

以上这些国际上不同学者的声音一则质疑中国比较文学建设的可能性，一则观望着这一学科在非西方国家的复兴样态。争议的声音不仅在国际学界，国内学界对于这一新兴学科的全局框架中涉及的理论、方法以及学科本身的立足点，例如前文所说的比较文学的定义，中国学派等等都处于持久论辩的漩涡。我们也通晓如果一直处于争议的漩涡中，便会被漩涡所吞噬，只有将论辩化为成果，才能转漩涡为涟漪，一圈一圈向外辐射，国际学人也在等待中国学者自己的声音。

上海交通大学王宁教授作为中国比较文学学者的国际发声者自 20 世纪末至今已撰文百余篇，他直言，全球化给西方学者带来了学科死亡论，但是中国比较文学必将在这全球化语境中更为兴盛，中国的比较文学学者一定会对国际文学研究做出更大的贡献。新世纪以来中国学者也不断地将自身的学科思考成果呈现在世界之前。2000 年，北京大学周小仪教授发文（*Comparative Literature in China*）[22]率先从学科史角度构建了中国比较文学在两个时期（20 世纪 20 年代至 50 年代，70 年代至 90 年代）的发展概貌，此文关于中国比较文学的复兴崛起是源自中国文学现代性的产生这一观点对美国芝加哥大学教授苏源熙（Haun Saussy）影响较深。苏源熙在 2006 年的专著 *Comparative Literature in an Age of Globalization* 中对于中国比较文学的讨论篇幅极少，其中心便是重申比较文学与中国文学现代性的联系。这篇文章也被哈佛大学教授大卫·达姆罗什（David Damrosch）收录于《普林斯顿比较文学资料手册》（*The Princeton Sourcebook in Comparative Literature*，2009[23]）。类似的学科史介绍在英语世界与法语世界都接续出现，以上大致反映了中国学者对于中国比较文学研究的大概描述在西学界的接受情况。学科史的构架对于国际学术对中国比较文学发展脉络的把握很有必要，但是在此基础上的学科理论实践才是关系于中国比较文学学科国际性发展的根本方向。

我在 20 世纪 80 年代以来 40 余年间便一直思考比较文学研究的理论构建问题，从以西方理论阐释中国文学而造成的中国文艺理论"失语症"思考

22 Zhou, Xiaoyi and Q.S. Tong, "Comparative Literature in China", Comparative Literature and Comparative Cultural Studies, ed., Totosy de Zepetnek, West Lafayette, Indiana: Purdue University Press, 2003, 268-283.

23 Damrosch, David (EDT)*The Princeton Sourcebook in Comparative Literature*: Princeton University Press

属于中国比较文学自身的学科方法论，从跨异质文化中产生的"文学误读""文化过滤""文学他国化"提出"比较文学变异学"理论。历经 10 年的不断思考，2013 年，我的英文著作：*The Variation Theory of Comparative Literature*（《比较文学变异学》），由全球著名的出版社之一斯普林格（Springer）出版社出版，并在美国纽约、英国伦敦、德国海德堡出版同时发行。*The Variation Theory of Comparative Literature*（《比较文学变异学》）系统地梳理了比较文学法国学派与美国学派研究范式的特点及局限，首次以全球通用的英语语言提出了中国比较文学学科理论新话语："比较文学变异学"。这一新概念、新范畴和新表述，引导国际学术界展开了对变异学的专刊研究（如普渡大学创办刊物《比较文学与文化》2017 年 19 期）和讨论。

欧洲科学院院士、西班牙圣地亚哥联合大学让·莫内讲席教授、比较文学系教授塞萨尔·多明戈斯教授（Cesar Dominguez），及美国科学院院士、芝加哥大学比较文学教授苏源熙（Haun Saussy）等学者合著的比较文学专著（Introducing Comparative literature: New Trends and Applications[24]）高度评价了比较文学变异学。苏源熙引用了《比较文学变异学》（英文版）中的部分内容，阐明比较文学变异学是十分重要的成果。与比较文学法国学派和美国学派形成对比，曹顺庆教授倡导第三阶段理论，即，新奇的、科学的中国学派的模式，以及具有中国学派本身的研究方法的理论创新与中国学派"（《比较文学变异学》（英文版）第 43 页）。通过对"中西文化异质性的"跨文明研究"，曹顺庆教授的看法会更进一步的发展与进步（《比较文学变异学》（英文版）第 43 页），这对于中国文学理论的转化和西方文学理论的意义具有十分重要的价值。（"Another important contribution in the direction of an imparative comparative literature-at least as procedure-is Cao Shunqing's 2013 *The Variation Theory of Comparative Literature*. In contrast to the "French School" and "American School" of comparative Literature, Cao advocates a "third-phrase theory", namely, "a novel and scientific mode of the Chinese school," a "theoretical innovation and systematization of the Chinese school by relying on our *own* methods" (*Variation Theory* 43; emphasis added). From this etic beginning, his proposal moves forward emically by developing a "cross-civilizaional study on the heterogeneity between

---

24 Cesar Dominguez,Haun Saussy,Dario Villanueva Introducing Comparative literature: New Trends and Applications，Routledge,2015

Chinese and Western culture" (43), which results in both the foreignization of Chinese literary theories and the Signification of Western literary theories.）

　　法国索邦大学（Sorbonne University）比较文学系主任伯纳德·弗朗科（Bernard Franco）教授在他出版的专著（《比较文学：历史、范畴与方法》）*La littératurecomparée: Histoire, domaines, méthodes* 中以专节引述变异学理论，他认为曹顺庆教授提出了区别于影响研究与平行研究的"第三条路"，即"变异理论"，这对应于观点的转变，从"跨文化研究"到"跨文明研究"。变异理论基于不同文明的文学体系相互碰撞为形式的交流过程中以产生新的文学元素，曹顺庆将其定义为"研究不同国家的文学现象所经历的变化"。因此曹顺庆教授提出的变异学理论概述了一个新的方向，并展示了比较文学在不同语言和文化领域之间建立多种可能的桥梁。（Il évoque l'hypothèse d'une troisième voie, la « théorie de la variation », qui correspond à un déplacement du point de vue, de celui des « études interculturelles » vers celui des « études transcivilisationnelles . » Cao Shunqing la définit comme « l'étude des variations subies par des phénomènes littéraires issus de différents pays, avec ou sans contact factuel, en même temps que l'étude comparative de l'hétérogénéité et de la variabilité de différentes expressions littéraires dans le même domaine ».Cette hypothèse esquisse une nouvelle orientation et montre la multiplicité des passerelles possibles que la littérature comparée établit entre domaines linguistiques et culturels différents.）<sup>25</sup>。

　　美国哈佛大学（Harvard University）厄内斯特·伯恩鲍姆讲席教授、比较文学教授大卫·达姆罗什（David Damrosch）对该专著尤为关注。他认为《比较文学变异学》（英文版）以中国视角呈现了比较文学学科话语的全球传播的有益尝试。曹顺庆教授对变异的关注提供了较为适用的视角，一方面超越了亨廷顿式简单的文化冲突模式，另一方面也跨越了同质性的普遍化。[26]国际学界对于变异学理论的关注已经逐渐从其创新性价值探讨延伸至文学研究，例如斯蒂文·托托西近日在 *Cultura* 发表的（Peripheralities: "Minor" Literatures, Women's Literature, and Adrienne Orosz de Csicser's Novels）一文中便成功地将变异学理论运用于阿德里安·奥罗兹的小说研究中。

---

25　Bernard Franco La littérature comparée: Histoire, domaines, méthodes, Armand Colin 2016.

26　David Damrosch Comparing the Literatures,Literary Studies in a Global Age,Princeton University Press,2020.

　　国际学界对于比较文学变异学的认可也证实了变异学作为一种普遍性理论提出的初衷，其合法性与适用性将在不同文化的学者实践中巩固、拓展与深化。它不仅仅是跨文明研究的方法，而是一种具有超越影响研究和平行研究，超越西方视角或东方视角的宏大视野、一种建立在文化异质性和变异性基础之上的融汇创生、一种追求世界文学和总体问题最终理想的哲学关怀。

　　以如此篇幅展现中国比较文学之况，是因为中国比较文学研究本就是在各种危机论、唱衰论的压力下，各种质疑论、概念论中艰难前行，不探源溯流难以体察今日中国比较文学研究成果之不易。文明的多样性发展离不开文明之间的交流互鉴。最具"跨文明"特征的比较文学学科更需要文明之间成果的共享、共识、共析与共赏，这是我们致力于比较文学研究领域的学术理想。

　　千里之行，不积跬步无以至，江海之阔，不积细流无以成！如此宏大的一套比较文学研究丛书得承花木兰总编辑杜洁祥先生之宏志，以及该公司同仁之辛劳，中国比较文学学者之鼎力相助，才可顺利集结出版，在此我要衷心向诸君表达感谢！中国比较文学研究仍有一条长远之途需跋涉，期以系列丛书一展全貌，愿读者诸君敬赐高见！

曹顺庆

二零二一年十月二十三日于成都锦丽园

# 目次

## 下　册

# 出版说明

　　《论语》是中华优秀传统文化的重要源头活水。《论语》中的许多词语已经成为中文语言系统里面的成语，一直活跃在我们的文字系统和日常口语中。如果有一本书能将这些成语汇集在一起，加以诠释和例解，对于普通读者的学习和应用一定大有裨益。

　　吴国珍先生的新书《出自一本书的180个成语》正是这样的一本书。这本书的出版，有助于加深对中国传统文化的认识。

　　《论语》中的词语进入成语范畴的，其实远不止该书所选的180个，只是其中的一些不仅在现代生活中已经极少出现，甚至连在早些年代的文言文中也已不复多见，比如"杞宋无征、告朔饩羊、犁生骍角、赐墙及肩"等等，尽管不少"成语大全"仍然予以收入，但实用机会可以说几乎全无，这些就没有收入在本书中了。

　　本书为收入的每个成语提供所在章节的原文，并有现代文今译和难字注释，且标明篇章，方便读者查阅原文以便深入学习。为了方便国外读者和国内英语爱好者，所引原文还配有英文翻译。这些英文出自作者早期出版的《论语最新英文全译全注本》。该书经孔子学院专家审阅，于2014年成为全球孔子学院的推荐读物，因而其英译是可信的。正文英译的下面紧接着是一条英文解读，目的是为国外读者解释该段原文的主旨或其背景知识。

　　由于年代的变迁，书中的一些成语的意思已有变化。作者注意到这一点，故如有必要，他会给每个成语配有两个英译。一般前一个接近原意，第二个接近新意。比如成语"文质彬彬"的英译现在常见的就有两种。一个是紧扣原文的 the proper combination of exterior refinement with plain nature，即"内在的质朴和外在的文采恰当地配合起来"。也就是说，为官者不但要本质好，而且要确保仪表、风度、言辞、礼节等外在的文雅，并且把两者恰当结合，才能达到很好的治理效果。但在现代文中，它纯粹是表示某人"很文雅"，故作者提供的另一个英译是 refined and elegant。

该书的另一个亮点是配有中英文例句。限于篇幅，作者给每个成语仅提供两个例句，但已经把每个成语可能出现的新旧用法都照顾到了。还是以"文质彬彬"为例，作者的例句是：

1. 古代要求当官者做到文质彬彬，以便树立威望。

Officials of ancient times were required to *combine their exterior refinement with plain nature properly* so as to build prestige.

2. 他只是工厂里的一名蓝领工人，外表却是文质彬彬的。

He is only a blue-collar worker at the factory, but he looks so *refined and elegant*.

在例 1 中，"文质彬彬"必须按原意翻译，方能体现其历史意蕴。在例 2 中，这个成语纯粹表示一个人很文雅的意思，为符合现代文意，必须做变通翻译，否则就会泥古不化而令人难以理解。

作者为编纂此书查阅了大量的中英文资料，作过较长时间的分析研究，力求使成语的今译符合辞书的传统解读，使其英译符合常见的译文，这有利于让本书与学校教材有较好的衔接。我们希望广大青少年及各类读者能喜欢这本书，并因此而喜欢上中国的传统的文化。

# The Publisher's Words

The *Analects of Confucius* is one of the sources of traditional Chinese culture. Many expressions in the book have become idioms in the Chinese linguistic system, and have been active in our writing system and daily spoken language. If, as many have expected, there is a book that includes all the idioms it has, it will be of great benefit to the readers who wish to learn and use them.

Mr. Wu Guozhen's new book, entitled *180 Idioms from One Single Book*, is such a book, and its publication now will help deepen the understanding of the traditional Chinese culture.

There are, in fact, more than those 180 idioms in the *Analects of Confucius*, except that some others are so rarely used in our modern life that the author does not include them in this book.

In this book, each idiom is furnished with the original text of the *Analects* from which it comes and the modern Chinese version of it. Each text is followed by a number to indicate its place in the book of the *Analects*. There are also English translation of the Chinese original texts. This will benefit English lovers at home as well as readers of other countries. The English translation is based on *A New Annotated English Version of the Analects of Confucius* created by Mr. Wu, which, after having been reviewed and approved by experts of the Confucius Institute Headquarters in 2014, has become the recommended reading of the Confucius Institutes worldwide. Each English translation is also followed by an English note which gives the main idea or background of the text.

Due to the changes of time, some of the idioms in the book have now changed in meaning. Having noticed that, the author provided two English translations for each idiom, one closely related to the original meaning and the other suiting its new variant. For example, there are two English translations of the idiom "文质彬彬". One is "the proper combination of exterior refinement with plain nature", which is closely related to the original text, meaning "the inner simplicity and the outer refinement are properly matched". That is to say, officials should not only be good in nature, but must also have external elegance such as appearance, demeanor, words and etiquette, and combine them properly so as to achieve good governance effects. However, in modern Chinese, it simply means "elegance", so another English translation provided by the author is "being refined and elegant".

Another merit of the book lies in the example sentences designed for each idiom. Due to limited space the author gave only two sentences for each, but they have covered the original meaning, and the variant meaning if any. Let's again take the idiom "文质彬彬" for example. We may say:

1. Officials of ancient times were required to *combine their exterior refinement with plain nature properly* so that they could build prestige.

Or we may say:

2. He is only a blue-collar worker at the factory, but he looks so refined and elegant.

As can be seen, Example 1 refers to things that happened in ancient China so the translation should be true to the original so that it will keep the historical meaning of this idiom.

As to Example 2, the variant meaning is used so the translation should be changed to suit its common use in our time. It will be hard to understand if we stick to its original meaning.

In order to compile the book, the author has looked through a large number of Chinese and English materials, and done a lot of analyses and researches, trying to make his modern Chinese paraphrases of the idioms conform to the traditional interpretation in the Chinese dictionaries, and his English translation conform to the traditional translation in some Chinese-English dictionaries. This will help align this book with other sources a reader may contact.

    We hope that readers of all ages will love this book, and thus love the traditional Chinese culture.

# 001　哀而不伤

a piteous mood free from excessive grief
mournful but not distressing
哀怨而不过度悲伤
悲哀而不痛苦

**【出处】**

子曰："《关雎》，乐而不淫，哀而不伤。"（论语 3.20）

The Master said, "The poem *Guanju* delivers a joyful passion free from indulgence, and a piteous mood free from excessive grief."

Note: *Guanju* is the first poem of the *Book of Poetry*. It depicts how a young man comes across a beautiful girl in an islet in a river and falls in love with her at first sight. Confucius highly praised the pure and innocent love between men and women shown in the poem, and pointed out at the same time that any feeling, whether of joy or grief, should not be displayed to its extreme.

**【今译】**

孔子说："《关雎》这篇诗，快乐而不过分放纵，哀怨而不过度悲伤。"

**【注释】**

1.《关雎》：即《国风·周南·关雎》，是中国古代第一部诗歌总集《诗经》中的第一首诗，通常认为是一首描写男女爱恋的情歌。

2. 淫：过多，过度，不适中。"不淫"跟下文的"不伤"均指喜怒哀乐有节制，合乎"中和"原则。

**【解读】**

《诗经》的诗早期都有配乐。孔子论诗，实质上是论乐。"音乐"在古代礼乐制度中起着至关重要的作用，有陶冶情操、和融社会的重要功能。"乐而不淫、哀而不伤"正好体现"乐主和"这一宗旨，符合"中正平和"的古代审美观。乐而不淫，指在享受诗歌音乐之美时心情愉悦却又不耽于其中而不可自拔；哀而不伤，指对社会的不公可以通过诗歌和音乐抒发哀怨或悲愤，却又不耽于极度的痛苦而难以自处。在后世，哀而不伤往往体现出一种身受痛苦而不沉浸于悲伤之中的坚强不屈的精神。

【句例】

1. 她的诗哀而不伤，其胸襟之博大令人赞叹。

Her poems *deliver a piteous mood free from excessive grief*, and the great breadth of her mind is highly appreciated.

2. 这部交响乐哀而不伤，反映了该国人民面对民族灾难时不屈不挠的精神。

This symphony, *mournful but not distressing*, reflects the unyielding spirit of the people of this country in face of a national disaster.

# 002　哀矜勿喜

to feel sad and sympathetic rather than joyful
to feel sad and sympathetic without gloating
（对罪犯）要感到悲哀和怜悯，不要（为自己的破案能力）沾沾自喜
对遭受灾祸的人要怜悯，不要幸灾乐祸

**【出处】**

曾子曰："上失其道，民散久矣。如得其情，则哀矜而勿喜。"（论语 19.19）

Zengzi said, "People have long been unruly because of bad governance of the ruler. So when you have managed to crack a criminal case, feel sad and sympathetic rather than joyful."

Note: Zengzi pointed out that in face of so many criminal cases caused by social injustice, a criminal judge should feel distressed and show sympathy for a criminal rather than be complacent about his ability in cracking the law cases. In our daily life today, this means that a person should not take pleasure in other people's misfortune.

**【今译】**

曾子说："在上位的人离开了正道，百姓早就散乱不羁了。如果你审出案情，就应当替（罪犯）感到悲哀并怜悯他们，而不要沾沾自喜（于自己的破案能力）。"

**【注释】**

1. 曾子：姓曾名参，孔子的重要弟子。

2. 上失其道：国君偏离正道，国家政局混乱。

3. 矜：怜悯，同情。

**【解读】**

此句讲乱世治民时法官们应有的一种心态。他们不该因为案件破得多而自鸣得意，而应该想想为什么会出现这种情况，要想到罪犯也是乱政的受害者，在不得已施以刑罚时要存一点怜悯心，更不能滥施刑罚。哀矜勿喜现在一

般指对遭受灾祸的人要怜悯，不要幸灾乐祸。

　　一个人在得意之时，往往最容易忘乎所以，对弱者和失败者缺乏同情心。因此，能不能面对他人的不幸而抱哀矜勿喜的心态，是对一个人道德修持的一种考验，身处顺境者容易忽视，须用心修炼。

【句例】

　　1. 罪犯最终受到了严惩，但法官告诫自己要哀矜勿喜。

Eventually the criminals were severely punished, but the judge warned himself that he should *feel sad and sympathetic* for them *rather than joyful* over his own ability in cracking the law case.

　　2. 对待敌对国家人民的灾难，我们应当抱着哀矜勿喜的正确心态。

To the people of a hostile country, we should be in such a correct mindset as to *feel sympathetic without gloating* over their mishap.

# 003　饱食终日，无所用心

to eat one's fill every day without applying
his mind to anything else
成天吃得饱饱的，什么心思也不用

【出处】

子曰："饱食终日，无所用心，难矣哉！不有博弈者乎？为之，犹贤乎已。"
（论语 17.22）

The Master said, "A man who simply eats his fill every day without applying
his mind to anything else will find it hard to get along! Aren't there things like games
or chess? Playing them might even be better than doing nothing at all."

Note: Confucius thought it wrong for some people to idle away all day and do nothing
serious. In the eyes of many people, playing games or chess is not a serious matter, but in the
eyes of Confucius, it is better than doing nothing at all. This shows how strongly Confucius
opposed the idle life.

【今译】

孔子说："成天吃得饱饱的，什么心思也不用，这种人日子真难混呀！不
是还有博彩和下棋的游戏吗？做做这样的事总比闲着好。"

【注释】

1. 博弈：博，一种称为"双陆"的游戏；弈，下棋，即下围棋。
2. 贤：好。

【解读】

这是孔子对那种饱食终日无所事事的人的批评。孔子本人对学习非常重
视，大部分时间都用来读书学习和实践，对自己的弟子也是如此要求。但对于
当时的一般人，只能退而求其次，降低要求。博弈是消遣性的游戏，经常做会
浪费时间，不利修身进学，所以此章重点不在孔子对博弈消遣的提倡，而在于
他对虚度时日的严重不认可和对虚度时日者的批评。

【句例】

1. 不像一些人退休后饱食终日无所用心，这位老科学家每天都要读书写文章。

Unlike some retired people who *eat their fill every day without applying their mind to anything else*, this old scientist keeps reading and writing every day.

2. 再这样饱食终日无所用心，我恐怕很快就会得老年痴呆症了。

If I continue to *eat my fill every day without applying my mind to anything else*, I'm afraid I'll soon suffer from Alzheimer's disease.

# 004　暴虎冯河

to fight a tiger barehanded and cross a river without a boat
to be reckless and in lack of strategy
空手搏虎，徒步涉水过河
莽撞而缺乏谋略

**【出处】**

子曰："暴虎冯河，死而无悔者，吾不与也。必也临事而惧。好谋而成者也。"（论语 7.11）

"With whom, Sir," asked Zilu, "would you work together in commanding a grand army?"

"I won't be working with those who would die without any regret in fighting a tiger barehanded, or crossing a river without a boat," replied the Master. "I certainly need one who is alert in face of danger and resorts to strategy for success."

Note: Confucius made the above reply when Zilu asked him with whom he would work together in commanding a grand army. Zilu was a good disciple who showed great valiancy in time of danger. But he was often reckless and in lack of strategy, so Confucius criticized him here. Confucius favored a combination of courage and strategy.

**【今译】**

孔子说："赤手空拳和老虎搏斗，徒步涉水过河，死了都不会后悔的人，我是不会和他共事的。我要共事的，一定要是遇事小心谨慎，善于谋划而能完成任务的人。"

**【注释】**

1. 暴虎：空拳赤手与老虎进行搏斗。

2. 冯（píng）河：（无船无桥而）徒步过河。

**【解读】**

在这句之前，子路问孔子说："如果老师您统帅一支大军，那么您愿意跟谁共事呢？"孔子作了以上的回答，实际上是暗含对子路有勇无谋的批评和告诫。子路是孔子最重要的弟子之一，他性格爽直，果敢刚烈，为人勇武，信守承诺，忠于职守。但孔子总觉得他的勇武有余而谋略不足。

【句例】

1. 这事要做成得靠谋略。我们总不能暴虎冯河，对吧？

We should resort to some strategy for success. We can't *fight a tiger barehanded, or cross a river without a boat*, right?

2. 他是个暴虎冯河之辈，恐怕不宜把这个任务交给他。

He is *reckless and in lack of strategy*, so I'm afraid we can't entrust this task with him.

# 005　博施济众

to benefit the people extensively and offer aid to all
to benefit the great majority
广泛地给人民施予恩惠，又能周济大众
惠及大众

【出处】

子贡曰："如有博施于民而能济众，何如？可谓仁乎？"子曰："何事于仁？必也圣乎！尧舜其犹病诸。"（论语 6.30）

Zigong said, "Let's suppose here's a man who extensively benefits the people and offers aid to all. What do you think of him? Can we say he is perfectly virtuous?"

"How can he be just perfectly virtuous?" said the Master. "He surely can be called a sage! Even Yao and Shun worried that they might not make it."

Note: Confucius pointed out that a man of perfect virtue should try to benefit the great majority of the people despite the fact that it was hard work even for an ancient sage king.

【今译】

子贡说："假若有一个人，他能广泛地给人民施予恩惠，又能周济大众，怎么样？可以算是仁人了吗？"孔子说："岂止是仁人，简直是圣人了！就连尧、舜也担心难以做到呢。"

【注释】

1. 施：施予恩惠，给予好处。

2. 病诸：担忧（做不到）这一点。病，担忧。

【解读】

孔子指出，君子应该努力造福于大多数人，即使对古代的圣王来说也是不容易做到。

【句例】

1. 一个好的领导人应该能博施济众，而不能仅仅对少数人施予小恩小惠。

A good leader should be able to *benefit the people extensively and offer aid to all*, but not just give some small favors to the minority.

2. 我只能捐这么一点点，离博施济众还差得远哪。

This is the very little that I could donate. It's still far from *benefiting the great majority.*

# 006 博文约礼

to broaden learning and regulate oneself with the rules of propriety
to learn extensively and regulate oneself with social norms
*广泛地学习古代的文化典籍，以礼来规范和约束自己，*
*广求学问，恪守社会规范*

【出处】

子曰："君子博学于文，约之以礼，亦可以弗畔矣夫。"（论语 6.27）

The Master said, "A superior man who keeps broadening his learning and regulating himself with the rules of propriety may not overstep what is right."

Note: Confucius pointed out that one would not go astray so long as he laid emphases on both academic studies and the observance of the rules of propriety (the topmost code of conduct).

【今译】

孔子说："君子广泛地学习古代的文化典籍，又以礼来约束自己，也就可以不离经叛道了。"

【注释】

1. 文：文化知识，指孔子教授的《诗》《书》《礼》《乐》《易》等经典。
2. 畔：同"叛"，指违背当时的礼法制度和传统。

【解读】

孔子提出"博学于文，约之以礼"作为教育学生的方法。"礼"是最高行为准则。孔子时代法纪制度尚未成型，社会成员以"礼"来规范和指导自己的思想和言行，这是培养君子人格的必由之路。"博学于文，约之以礼"由后世概括为"博文约礼"，已成为一些重要教育机构的口号。

【句例】

1. 只有做到博文约礼，才能成为德才兼备的知识分子。

Only by *learning extensively and regulating himself with social norms* can a person become an intellectual with both ability and moral integrity.

2. 香港中文大学的校训是"博文约礼"。

The motto of the Chinese University of Hong Kong is "*Through learning and temperance to virtue*".

# 007　博学笃志

to broaden one's learning and firmly remember what is learned
to learn extensively and have good memory
博览群书，扩展学问，牢牢记住所学过的东西
广泛学习，记忆力强

**【出处】**

子夏曰："博学而笃志，切问而近思，仁在其中矣。"（论语 19.6）

Zixia said, "Broaden your learning and firmly remember what is learned, ask questions of immediate concern and ponder over things closely around, and you are on the way to moral perfection."

Note: Benevolence is a proper noun that reflects the core value of Confucianism. Roughly equivalent to moral perfection but far more than that, it is the highest realm of thought that is hard for most people to reach. Still, Confucius encouraged people to learn extensively and do good every day to try to be close to it. Zixia required his disciples to study extensively and focus on issues closely related to them, saying that by doing this they would be close to benevolence.

**【今译】**

子夏说："博览群书，扩展学问，牢牢记住所学过的东西，提出切身的问题，思考身边的事物，仁就在其中了。"

**【注释】**

1. 笃志：牢记。笃，厚实、结实；志，同"识"（zhì），记住。

**【解读】**

"仁"仁是体现儒家核心价值的专有名词。大致相当于道德上的完美，但远不止于此。它是大多数人难以企及的最高思想境界。尽管如此，孔子还是鼓励人们广泛地学各种知识，坚持每天做好事，尽量靠近它。子夏要求他的弟子广泛学习，专注于与他们密切相关的问题，他认为坚持这样做他们就接近仁。

**【句例】**

1. 学生时代他博学笃志，这为他多年后的学术研究打下坚实的基础。

As a student he *learned extensively and remembered what he learned firmly*. This helped to lay a solid foundation for his academic research many years later.

2. 他从小博学笃志，志存高远，成年后为中国的科技事业作出极大的贡献。

When young he *learnt extensively and had good memory*, and had lofty ambition. When he grew up, he made great contributions to China's science and technology.

# 008 不耻下问

to feel no shame in consulting one's inferiors
do not feel ashamed to learn from the less competent
不以向自己的下级请教为耻
不以向能力较低的人请教为耻

**【出处】**

子曰："敏而好学，不耻下问，是以谓之文也。"（论语 5.15）

The Master said, "He was bright and keen on learning; he felt no shame in consulting his inferiors! That's why his posthumous title is WEN."

Note: Confucius explained why Kongwenzi was worthy of the posthumous title "WEN". In ancient China, a king or an important official would be given a posthumous title when he died to sum up his merits or demerits. "WEN" was the best title one could get, meaning excellent in virtue, keen on learning, eager to consult the inferior and kind and beneficial to the people.

**【今译】**

孔子说："他聪敏勤勉而好学，不以向比他地位卑下的人请教为耻，所以给他谥号叫'文'。"

**【注释】**

1. 下问：向下级或比自己差的人请教。

2. 文：古代帝王和高官去世后得到的谥号。"文"是高度赞美的谥号，有"道德博闻、学勤好问、慈惠爱民"等含义。

**【解读】**

本句之前，孔子的学生子贡问孔子说：孔文子（卫国大夫孔圉）的学问及才华虽然很高，但是比他更杰出的人还很多，凭什么赐给他'文'这么高的称号？孔子解释说孔文子敏而好学、不耻下问，这就属于"文"的谥号中的内容。

【句例】

1. 他身居高位而不耻下问，所以不但了解下情，而且知识面不断拓宽。

Although he is in a high position, he *feels no shame in consulting those in inferior positions*. Thus he not only knows about the situation at the lower levels, but also keeps broadening his knowledge scope.

2. 他一向不耻下问，所以很多方面都进步很快。

He used not to *feel ashamed to learn from the less competent*, so he made rapid progress in many aspects.

# 009 不得其门而入

cannot find the door to get in
cannot find a proper approach
找不到门，走不进去，
找不到合适的途径

## 【出处】

子贡曰："譬之宫墙，赐之墙也及肩，窥见室家之好。夫子之墙数仞，不得其门而入，不见宗庙之类，百官之富。"（论语 19.23）

Zigong said, "Let me take a bounding wall for example. My wall reaches only to the shoulder. One may peep over it, and see all the beauty in my apartment. The bounding wall of my Master's house is metres high. If one does not find the gate to enter it, he can see neither the magnificence of the ancestral temple nor the splendor of the mansions within."

Note: Some people said Zigong was better than his teacher Confucius. Zigong refuted them, saying that people knew little about the greatness of Confucius simply because they knew little about his great doctrine. For this he gave a metaphor: People outside a tall bounding wall could not see things in a great house if they found no way to enter it, meaning that Confucius' doctrine was too profound for some people to get access to.

## 【今译】

子贡说："拿围墙来作比喻，我家的围墙只有齐肩高，里面漂亮的房屋可以看得一清二楚。老师家的围墙却有几仞高，如果找不到门进去，你就看不见里面宗庙的富丽堂皇和房屋的绚丽多彩。"

## 【注释】

1. 子贡：端木赐，字子贡，孔子的重要弟子。

2. 仞：古代长度单位，一仞约等于七尺或八尺。

3. 官：此处是"馆"的意思。

【解读】

本句之前，有人说子贡比孔子好。子贡反驳说，因为自己的德行比较浅薄，容易被人理解，就像围墙低，里面只要有点好的东西，都会让外面的人一览无余，而孔子博大精深，不易被人理解，就像围墙高，里面的馆舍再美，如果没进门去，那就什么也看不见。子贡以此借喻很多人没机会深入了解孔子，看不出孔子的伟大。从这里也可以看出子贡的谦虚和明理。

【句例】

1. 他们终于在悬崖边找到一座古堡，但摸索了半天却不得其门而入。

They finally found an old castle on the edge of the cliff. They groped for a long time but *could not find a door to get in*.

2. 他们一直试图破解这个密码，却不得其门而入。

They had been trying to crack the code, but *could not find a proper approach*.

# 010　不得其死

do not die a natural death
to die an abnormal death
do not die in bed
不能自然寿终，
非正常死亡

**【出处】**

子曰："若由也，不得其死然。"（论语 11.13）

The Master said, "A man like Zhong You might not die a natural death."

Note: Confucius was happy when he was chatting with some of his worthy disciples. But he was worried about Zilu, his adventurous disciple. Later, Zilu did die a heroic death in fighting to protect his superior, which caused Confucius to be over-grieved.

**【今译】**

孔子说："像仲由这样，只怕得不到善终吧！"

**【注释】**

1. 由：姓仲名由，字子路，孔子最重要的弟子之一。

2. 不得其死然：不得善终，不能自然寿终。

**【解读】**

本句之前，孔子在闲谈时对闵子侍、冉有和子路（仲由）三位高徒进行评价。孔子对子路的评价尤其显示其先见之明。子路好勇而刚，刚而易折，性格决定命运，孔子的话隐含对这位正直忠勇的弟子的担忧和惋惜。事实不幸证实了孔子的预言，子路果然在一次护主的格斗中死得非常惨烈。

**【句例】**

1. 这个匪徒很清楚，他注定不得其死。

The mobster knew very well that he was doomed to *die an abnormal death*.

2. 在中华文化里，人们希望能寿终正寝。不得其死被认为是人生的缺憾。

In Chinese culture, people hope to *die a natural death. Not to die in bed* is considered by them to be a failure of life.

# 011  不愤不启　不悱不发

do not give enlightenment unless (a student) has racked
his brains and yet fails to understand
do not tell (a student) how to speak unless he has tried hard
to express himself but fails to open his mouth
不到（学生）想弄明白而实在弄不明白的时候不去开导他
不到（学生）想说而实在说不出来的时候不去启发他

【出处】

子曰："不愤不启，不悱不发。"（论语 7.8）

The Master said, "Never give (a student) enlightenment unless he has racked his brains and yet fails to understand, or unless he has tried hard to express himself but fails to open his mouth."

Note: This reveals Confucius' heuristic method in teaching. Confucius meant that only when the learner had a very strong desire to get to know a thing would he begin to explain it to him.

【今译】

孔子说："不到学生想弄明白而实在弄不明白的时候，不去开导他；不到他想说而实在说不出来的时候，不去启发他。"

【注释】

1. 愤：苦思冥想而仍然领会不了的样子。
2. 悱：想说又不能明确说出来的样子。

【解读】

本句讲孔子以启发式教育充分调动学生学习上的主观能动性。学习者的心理特点是：通过自己心理欲望求得的知识，往往更能牢记不忘。求知的欲望越强烈，求得的过程越曲折，脑中的记忆就越牢固。孔子深谙这一心理特点并应用到学生的身上，传授了这历两千余年而不衰的启发式教育方法，至今还在显示其强大的生命力。

【句例】

1. 我们的老师坚持不愤不启的原则，不会轻易为我们讲解。

Our teacher stuck to the principle on which he would not readily *give us enlightenment unless we had racked our brains yet failed to understand.*

2. 我对她可谓不悱不发，那可是为了她好。

I *would not tell her how to speak unless she tried hard to express herself but failed to open her mouth*. I should say that was for her good.

# 012   不改其乐

Nothing can take away one's delight in life.
never change one's delight in something
没有什么能带走一个人的生活乐趣。
不改变某一方面的乐趣

**【出处】**

子曰："贤哉回也，一箪食，一瓢饮，在陋巷，人不堪其忧，回也不改其乐。"（论语 6.11）

The Master said, "Virtuous indeed is Yan Hui! A small bamboo basket of food, a gourd of water, and a humble dwelling in the backstreet, which are unbearable for others, never take away his delight in life."

Note: Confucius highly appreciated his best disciple Yan Hui for his love of learning and delight in life though he was in great adversity.

**【今译】**

孔子说："颜回的品质是多么高尚啊！吃的是一小竹筐小米粥，喝的是一瓢清水，住的是偏僻的后街小巷，别人都忍受不了这种穷困清苦，颜回却没有改变他人生的乐趣。"

**【注释】**

1. 不改其乐：不改变对人生乐趣的追求。这里的"乐"即"孔颜之乐"，指在艰难困顿的情况下坚持读书学习修身，并把治国平天下的理想作为人生最美好的追求。

**【解读】**

此段记孔子盛赞其高徒颜回一事。颜回极贫，但谦虚好学，崇德向仁，安贫乐道，而孔子这一盛赞，也因此引出"孔颜之乐"这一千古话题。孔子和颜回究竟乐什么，历来众说纷纭，但有一点是肯定的，那是一种精神多于物质的快乐，是读书学习带来的求知欲望的满足，是人生目标的追求带来的精神慰藉，是师生之情带来的愉悦。在这些人生乐趣中，读书学习应该摆在首位。他们读的是圣贤的教诲，是古代历史和治国方略，并憧憬着有一天用所学知识来为世所用，这是他们身处窘困之中的巨大精神支柱。

【句例】

1. 那位科学家生前一直是贫病交加，但他从来也不改其乐。

That scientist had been plagued by poverty and illness during his lifetime, but it *never took away his delights in life*.

2. 家父热衷于古代书籍的收藏，一生不改其乐。

My father was keen on collecting ancient books, and for all his life he *never changed his delight in it*.

# 013　不教而杀

to impose death penalty without giving jural instructions beforehand
a death penalty or punishment without a prior warning
不经事先教育便加以杀戮，
未经事先警示便加以杀戮或惩处

【出处】

子曰："不教而杀谓之虐。"（论语 20.2）

The Master said, "To impose death penalty without giving jural instructions beforehand—that is called cruelty."

Note: Confucius pointed out that officials had the responsibility to give the people jural instruction for the crime prevention, and warned them not to resort to punishment without education.

【今译】

孔子说："不经事先教育便加以杀戮，这是在行虐。"

【注释】

1. 教：教育，管教。

2. 虐：暴虐，做暴虐的事。

【解读】

此句记子张向孔子请教为官从政的要领，孔子提出了好几个值得注意的方面，这里仅仅是其中的一句。这句话意在告诉为官者，他们负有对民众实施礼乐和法治教育的责任，不能事先不加教育管教，事发后滥施刑罚。这是孔子重德教、轻刑罚思想的具体体现。

【句例】

1. 不教而杀，这不是政府制定法律的本意。

It is not the intention of the government to make laws to *impose death penalty without giving jural instructions beforehand.*

2. 仅仅迟到一次就开除，这简直是不教而杀！

To dismiss one for being late only once! This is as bad as *a death penalty without a prior warning.*

# 014　不堪其忧

*to be unbearable*
*cannot bear the wretched plight*
*无法忍受*
*无法忍受某种困顿*

**【出处】**

子曰："一箪食，一瓢饮，在陋巷，人不堪其忧，回也不改其乐。"（论语 6.11）

The Master said, "A bamboo basket of food, a gourd of water, and a humble dwelling in the backstreet, which are unbearable for others, never take away Yan Hui's delights in life."

Note: Confucius highly appreciated his best disciple Yan Hui for his love of learning and delight in life though he was in great adversity.

**【今译】**

孔子说，"吃的是一小竹筐小米粥，喝的是一瓢清水，住的是偏僻的后街小巷，别人都忍受不了这种穷困清苦，颜回却没有改变他人生的乐趣。"

**【注释】**

1. 箪：古代盛饭的小竹筐。
2. 忧：愁苦，困苦。

**【解读】**

孔子赞扬颜回忍受他人无法忍受的困苦，坚持读书学习、修身养德，希望有一天能为国为民服务的精神。

另外，"不堪其忧"不要写成"不堪其扰"。后者是"受不了那种搅扰（骚扰、打扰）"的意思，是一个普通词语而非成语。

【句例】

1. 别人身处那种困境往往不堪其忧，他却能泰然处之。

While others might *be unbearable* in that adversity, he would bear it with equanimity.

2. 这个社区没水没电，居民们实在不堪其忧。

There is no water or electricity supply in this neighborhood, and the residents really *cannot bear the wretched plight*.

# 015 不念旧恶

to forgive and forget
to bear no past grudge
to forgive the wrong done by others
不计较过去的仇怨
不计前嫌

**【出处】**

子曰："伯夷叔齐不念旧恶，怨是用希。"（论语 5.23）

The Master said, "Boyi and Shuqi forgave and forgot. Thus they had little hatred."

Note: Sometimes to forget the past hatred is to lead a person out of his spiritual shackles. Thus Confucius praised Boyi and Shuqi in this aspect.

**【今译】**

孔子说："伯夷、叔齐两个人不记旧仇，因此，心中的怨恨也就少了。"

**【注释】**

1. 伯夷、叔齐：殷朝末年孤竹君的两个儿子。相传其父遗命要立叔齐为继承人。孤竹君死后，叔齐要让位给大哥伯夷，伯夷不受，叔齐也不愿继位，两人先后逃往周国。周武王起兵伐纣，他们认为这是以臣弑君，是不忠行为，曾加以拦阻。周灭商统一天下后，他们不食周粟（以吃周朝的粮食为耻），逃进深山中以野草充饥，饿死在首阳山中。

2. 用：因此。

**【解读】**

孔子以伯夷、叔齐为例说明人必须不念旧恶才能减少怨恨。伯夷和叔齐究竟不计较谁的怨仇，孔子这里没有明讲。有人说是对暴君纣王而言，有的说是对武王伐纣的所谓"以下犯上"的怨怼，但两例都没有证据，本身也缺乏说服力。不过，就词论词，孔子这一不计前嫌消弭怨恨的教导也成了后世处理人际关系的一个准则。

【句例】

1. 对于侵略者的种种暴行，在他们彻底认罪之前，我们很少人能做到不念旧恶。

For the atrocities of the aggressors, few of us would be able to *forgive and forget* before they make utter confession of guilt.

2. 人非圣贤，孰能无过。对他给我造成的冤屈，我其实已经不念旧恶了。

To err is human. I've actually chosen to *forget the wrong done to me* by him.

# 016　不辱使命

do not fail a mission entrusted by others
to live up to one's mission
不辜负别人交给的差使
能完成某一项任务

**【出处】**

子贡问曰："何如斯可谓之士矣？"子曰："行己有耻，使于四方，不辱君命，可谓士矣。"（论语 13.20）

Zigong asked Confucius, "What should scholars do in order to be worthy of the title?" The Master said, "They should maintain a sense of shame in their conduct, and when dispatched to other states, never fail a mission entrusted by their sovereign. In this way they may deserve the title scholar."

Note: Confucius tried to grade scholars in his time. According to him, the highest grade of scholars should be those who could accomplish something great for the state, and those who could correctly exercise the duty endowed by the state in international association and do things in the interests of the state.

**【今译】**

子贡问道："怎样做才可以称得上是士呢？"孔子说："做事时有知耻之心，出使其他国家，能不辜负君主交付的使命，可以叫做士。"

**【注释】**

1. 不辱君命：不辜负国君交给的使命；认真完成国君交给的任务。现在一般改为"不辱使命"。

**【解读】**

这是孔子对士提出的要求。春秋时期，士作为治国的辅助力量已经崛起。孔子把士的表现的高低分为几个不同层次。能做到"使于四方不辱君命"的士，是属于治国平天下层次的最高一级的士，他们能在国际交往中正确地行使国家赋予的职责，做事符合国家的利益。

【句例】

1. 作为一名外交大臣他精明干练，从来不辱使命。

As a foreign minister he was capable and well-experienced, and *never failed the mission* entrusted by the state.

2. 这回总经理助理可谓不辱使命，成功地争取到银行贷款。

This time the assistant general manager succeeded in securing the bank loans. He can be said to *have lived up to his mission.*

# 017  不舍昼夜

day and night without cease
round the clock
unceasingly
不分白天和黑夜，没有停息
不停地

【出处】

子在川上曰："逝者如斯夫，不舍昼夜。"（论语 9.17）

Watching the surging current by the riverside the Master said, "O time elapses just like this, day and night without cease!"

Note: When Confucius was standing by the riverside watching the water flowing forward swiftly and endlessly, he expressed his emotion something like "Lost time is never found again", and "Time and tide wait for no man".

【今译】

孔子站在河边感慨地说："时光的流逝就像这河水一样，不分昼夜地流淌啊!"

【注释】

1. 逝者：一般认为是指逝去的时光，也指人世间过去了的一切事物，比如个人的所作所为、功名利禄，或国家的盛衰兴替。

2. 不舍昼夜：不分白天和黑夜。舍，放弃，停止。

【解读】

这是孔子对韶光易逝的感慨，这里既有对世间一切事物盛衰兴替的感慨，也有鞭策人们珍惜光阴、只争朝夕，努力争取成就一番事业的含义。他的话也成了"时不我待"的警语。

【句例】

1. 这个工厂发出严重噪音，不舍昼夜，周边群众不堪其扰。

The factory was making terrible noises, *day and night without cease*, and the people around could hardly bear it.

2. 工人们不舍昼夜连续工作了一个月，终于提前完成了任务。

The workers had been working *round the clock* for a month, and finally fulfilled the task ahead of schedule.

# 018　不亦乐乎

isn't it delightful
very, very much
不是很快乐吗
很、非常

**【出处】**

子曰："有朋自远方来，不亦乐乎？"（论语 1.1）

The Master said, "Isn't it delightful to have friends coming from afar?"

Note: This sentence comes from the first chapter of the *Analects of Confucius*. Confucius taught his disciples how to learn and how to make friends. Here he emphasized the word delightful, hoping the disciples would experience the happiness of learning and growing, and feel the joy of social life. Once teenagers have such an opportunity to learn and get together, they will naturally be happy, and have a good start in their life.

**【今译】**

孔子说："有朋友从远方来，不是很令人高兴吗？"

**【注释】**

1. 不亦乐乎：不是很快乐吗。有时也可以用来表示很、非常的意思，是一种诙谐的用法。

**【解读】**

本句出自论语首章，记孔子对其弟子在为学、交友、涵养等方面的教诲。对于为学和交友，孔子突出"悦、乐"二字，是要让前来求学的弟子体验学习和成长的快乐，感受处世的愉悦。青少年一旦拥有这样的机会，自然快乐愉悦，人生就必然有一个良好的开端。

**【句例】**

1. 天气甚佳，来个乡间远足不亦乐乎？

*Isn't it delightful* to make an excursion into the countryside on such a fine day?

2. 我们这边忙得不亦乐乎，他们却在那边吵得不亦乐乎。

While we are *very* busy here, they are quarreling there *very* heatedly.

# 019  不在其位，不谋其政

Those who do not hold the position shall not
involve themselves in its affairs.
do not do things beyond one's remit
不在那个职位上，就不过问与那个职位有关的事
不做超出职权范围的事

**【出处】**

子曰："不在其位，不谋其政。"（论语 8.14）

The Master said, "He who does not hold the position shall not involve himself in its affairs."

Note: This is an important principle to avoid exceeding one's authority in office. In any society, each official is required to stand in his place performing his own duty, and then the whole system will function well.

**【今译】**

孔子说："不在那个职位上，就不过问与那个职位有关的事。"

**【注释】**

1. 谋其政：过问那职务范围内的事。

**【解读】**

"不在其位，不谋其政"这一说法涉及到儒家所注重的名分问题。如果不在其位而谋其政，那就会名不正而言不顺，有僭越之嫌，在今天看来也不符合居官各司其职的普世原则。这里说的"谋其政"仅仅是指官员在职务范围内应做的工作，但后世把"谋其政"说成是老百姓对政治的关心，认为孔子反对老百姓关心政治。这种说法把"谋其政"跟"关心政治"等同起来，犯了混淆概念的错误。其实，即便在现代社会，百姓可以充分关心国家大事，但也是不能直接参与谋划政事的。

【句例】

1. 恕我无法帮你们完成工程筹款。不在其位，不谋其政，这点你是清楚的。

Sorry I can't help you with the project fundraising. You know *I do not hold the position and should not involve myself in this affair.*

2. 我让十五岁的儿子帮他妈妈刷碗，他竟然说什么不在其位，不谋其政。

I told my 15-year-old son to help his mother wash the dishes, and he went so far as to say he *wouldn't do things beyond his remit.*

# 020　不知而作

to be ignorant yet want to create something
to say or write what one knows nothing about
什么都不懂却在那里随意编造，
说或写自己不懂的东西

【出处】

子曰："盖有不知而作之者，我无是也。多闻，择其善者而从之，多见而识之，知之次也。"（论语 7.28）

The Master said, "There may be some who are ignorant yet want to create something, but I am not one of them. I listen to different views and choose what is good to follow. I observe different things and keep them in mind. Such is the second best way of learning.

Note: Confucius warned his disciples not to try to create anything before they really possessed enough knowledge, and suggested a down-to-earth attitude in this aspect. That is, to seek knowledge gradually through constant observing and learning and selective acceptance.

【今译】

孔子说："有这样一种人，可能他什么都不懂却在那里随意编造，我却没有这样做过。多听，选择其中好的来学习；多看，然后记在心里，这是仅次于生而知之的求知办法。"

【注释】

1. 不知而作：什么都不懂，却在那里随意编造。

2. 识：同"志"，记住。

3. 知之次：次一等的认知方法。

【解读】

孔子提倡对自己不知道的东西，应该多闻、多见，努力学习，反对那种本来什么都不懂，却在那里凭空创作或讲述的做法。这是他对自己的要求，同时也要求他的学生这样去做。而要避免"不知而作"，唯一的办法就是求知。一般人认为，最高等的认知是"生而知之"，但那实际上是不可能的，而"学而知之"作为次一等的认知方法，才是最现实的求知途径。

【句例】

1. 他不知而作，写出来的历史故事成了笑柄。

He is *ignorant yet wants to create something*, so the historical story he wrote has become a laughing stock.

2. 我们在动笔之前尽量查了各种各样的资料，以避免不知而作。

We tried to look up all kinds of information before we started so as to avoid *writing what we knew nothing about*.

# 021 不知老之将至

to care little about the increasing age
unaware of the approaching of old age
to forget one is getting old
*不知自己快老了*
*忘掉了自己的衰老*

**【出处】**

子曰："其为人也，发愤忘食，乐以忘忧，不知老之将至云尔。"（论语 7.19）

The Master, "I am no more than a man who forgets his food when racking his brains without a result, who forgets his worries while taking delight in life, and who cares little about the increasing age."

Note: When someone asked Zilu what Confucius was like, Zilu did not know how to answer, and Confucius told him to give the above answer. That was also the self-evaluation of Confucius. In his later years, Confucius was able to concentrate on teaching and focus on reformatting some ancient books. Therefore, he was in a happy mood, and was still working hard without knowing that he was getting old.

**【今译】**

孔子（讲到自己时）说："他这个人呐，陷于苦思冥想而不得要领之时，连饭都会忘记吃；沉浸在快乐之中而忘掉忧虑，就连自己快老了都不知道，如此而已。"

**【注释】**

1. 发愤：苦思冥想而领会不了的样子。
2. 云尔：如此而已。

**【解读】**

当有人问子路孔子是个怎么样的人时，子路不知该如何回答，孔子就告诉他可以作以上的应答。那也是孔子的自我评价。晚年的孔子一方面专心教学，一方面专注于古籍的整理，能从心所欲，故心情愉快，不顾已经步入了衰老期，依然在忘情地奋斗着。

【句例】

1. 王先生不知老之将至，七十岁才开始把《易经》译成荷兰语。

*Caring little about his increasing age*, Mr. Wang began to translate the *Book of Changes* into Dutch when he turned seventy.

2. 这群老科学家夜以继日地研究生物医学，全然不知老之将至。

These senior scientists work day and night to make research on biomedicine, completely *unaware of the approaching of old age*.

# 022　察言观色

*to judge others' words and read their faces*
*to observe somebody's speech and countenance*
揣摩别人的话语，观察别人的脸色
观察他人的言语和脸部的神情

## 【出处】

子曰："夫达也者，质直而好义，察言而观色，虑以下人。"（论语 12.20）

The Master said, "A distinguished man is upright in nature and has the sense of justice. He is good at judging other people's words and reading their faces, and tries to be humble to others."

Note: Confucius talked about how a scholar could be distinguished in a state, and said that one of his fine qualities should be to try to be humble to others. In order to be humble to others, one should be good at judging other people's words and reading their faces, and made correct responses after that.

## 【今译】

孔子说："所谓显达，那是要品质正直，遵从礼义，善于揣摩别人的话语，观察别人的脸色，经常想着以谦卑的姿态待人。"

## 【注释】

1. 察：详审，仔细观察。
2. 虑以下人：虑，考虑，想着。下人，谦卑待人。

## 【解读】

讲到一个士人如何才能做到"达"（显达），孔子认为其中一条就是要能够谦卑待人。而要谦卑待人，就要善于揣摩别人的话语，观察别人的脸色，及时作出正确的反应。

## 【句例】

1. 通过察言观色，我很快发现她得了一种难以启口的疾病。

By *judging her words and reading her face*, I soon discovered that she was suffering from an unutterable disease.

2. 心理医生必须具备极高察言观色的能力。

A psychologist must have great abilities to *observe others' speech and countenance*.

# 023　成人之美

to help or support others to fulfill their nice wishes

*帮助他人实现美好愿望*

【出处】

子曰："君子成人之美，不成人之恶。小人反是。"（论语 12.16）

The Master said, "A virtuous man helps others to fulfill their nice wishes but not their evil ones. A base man does the opposite."

Note: A virtuous man likes others to be good so they will try to support others in achieving their worthy goals, either substantially or, most often, morally and spiritually. A virtueless man is evil-minded so he would love to support others in achieving their evil goals.

【今译】

孔子说："君子成全别人的好事，而不助长别人的恶行。小人则与此相反。"

【注释】

1. 成人之美：成全别人的好事，指赞成、支持、帮助别人实现其美好的愿望。

2. 成人之恶：促成别人的坏事，指看到别人干坏事而不加以制止，甚至助其一把。

【解读】

君子总是从善良的和有利于他人的愿望出发，希望促使别人实现美好的愿望和正当的要求。君子看到别人在做一件坏事，当然不会支持，而是加以劝阻，绝对不会推波助澜。小人的做派刚好相反，他们容不得别人做得好，总要加以破坏，让别人达不到美好的愿望。而当他们看到别人做坏事时，往往幸灾乐祸，甚至曲意逢迎，促使人往错误的道路滑得更远。

【句例】

1. 既然你那么喜欢那幅古画，我就不再出价与你竞标了。君子成人之美嘛。

Since you like the ancient painting so much, I will no longer bid for it. A gentleman should *support others to fulfill their nice wishes*.

2. 我知道她不爱我，而是更爱振明，还真心想要同他结婚，于是便主动离开她，以便成人之美。

I knew that instead of loving me, she loved Zhenming better, and really hoped to marry him, so I chose to leave her voluntarily so as to *help them to fulfill their nice wish*.

# 024　从心所欲

to follow what one's heart desires
to do something as one wishes
to do whatever one desires to do
随心所欲，按自己的心愿行事
做自己想做的事

【出处】

子曰："七十而从心所欲不逾矩。"（论语 2.4）

The Master said, "In my seventies I can follow what my heart desires without transgressing what is right."

Note: Confucius described how he gradually grew up at different ages toward the perfection of his personality. He said by the age of seventy, he had reached the highest level of morality and was free to do what he loved without making a mistake.

【今译】

孔子说："我七十岁能随心所欲而不越出规矩。"

【注释】

1. 逾矩：逾越规矩。

【解读】

这一章孔子描述他在不同年龄的成长过程。对他来说，到了七十岁，由于经历过无数的坎坷和磨练，其个人的道德修养已经达到了最高的境界，思想和行为已经能符合外界的客观规律，从而能够左右逢源，得心应手，做自己希望做的事而不逾越规矩。

【句例】

1. 忙碌了大半辈子，王先生希望退休后能从心所欲，过一个有意义的晚年。

Having been busy for the better half of his life, Mr. Wang hopes to retire and *do something as he wishes* so as to lead a meaningful life in his late years.

2. 人是社会动物，要受各种因素的制约，所以有时很难事事都能够从心所欲。

Men are social animals that are subject to all kinds of factors, so sometimes it is difficult for them to *do whatever they desire to do*.

# 025  待价而沽

to wait to sell it to a wise buyer
to wait to sell it at a high price
等待好买主
等待高价才出卖

【出处】

子贡曰："有美玉于斯，韫椟而藏诸？求善贾而沽诸？"子曰："沽之哉，沽之哉！我待贾者也。（论语 9.13）

Zigong asked Confucius, "Let's suppose there is a beautiful jade here. Shall we keep it in a casket, or seek to sell it to a wise buyer?"

"Sell it! Oh, sell it!" responded the Master. "I am expecting such a buyer."

Note: Confucius had great talents in state administration, and hoped that he could "sell" his doctrine to a state ruler so that he would have the opportunity to use it. Many state rulers admired him but were not going to use him, and he was disappointed and felt quite helpless, so now he was anxious to find an opportunity.

【今译】

子贡说："这里有一块美玉，是把它收藏在匣子里呢？还是找一个识货的商人卖掉呢？"孔子说："卖掉吧，卖掉吧！我正在等着识货的买主呢。"

【注释】

1. 沽：买，卖。

2. 待价而沽：等待好价格才卖出去。一般指卖物品，有时也指寻找机会以自己的才华或良策等为他人所用并获取高利。

【解读】

孔子 54 岁后离开鲁国周游列国，期待把他以仁德礼乐治天下的学说"卖"给诸侯国君以便实施，却始终难以如愿，于是有时也难免有急于出手的情绪。这是对孔子求仕心切的生动描述。孔子要让自己的学说得以实施，必须做官，久而机会不自至，焦虑之情油然而生，才会有以上的师生对话。"待价而沽"在旧时常比喻等待时机出来做官，现在多比喻等待有好的待遇或条件才答应出来任职或做事。

**【句例】**

1. 那个收藏家知道他的青花瓷大花瓶价值连城，所以决定待价而沽。

The collector knew that his big blue and white porcelain vase was priceless, so he decided to *wait to sell it to a wise buyer*.

2. 他自视甚高，所以在求职时决定待价而沽，找个一流的公司。

He thought so highly of himself that he decided to *wait and "sell" himself at a high price* to a first-rate company.

# 026 箪食瓢饮

a small bamboo basket of food and a gourd of water
to live an extremely poor life
吃的是一小竹筐小米粥，喝的是一瓢清水
过极端贫困的生活

**【出处】**

子曰："贤哉回也，一箪食，一瓢饮，在陋巷，人不堪其忧，回也不改其乐。"（论语 6.11）

The Master said, "Virtuous indeed is Yan Hui! A small bamboo basket of food, a gourd of water, and a humble dwelling in the backstreet, which are unbearable for others, never take away his delights in life."

Note: Confucius was here praising his best disciple Yanhui. Yan Hui was extremely poor, and led an extremely hard life, but he studied very hard, and had self-cultivation constantly so as to improve his moral level. He worked with his teacher hoping to seek for a chance to save the state and the people in the troubled time.

**【今译】**

孔子说："颜回的品质是多么高尚啊！吃的是一小竹筐小米粥，喝的是一瓢清水，住的是偏僻的后街小巷，别人都忍受不了这种穷困清苦，颜回却没有改变他人生的乐趣。"

**【注释】**

1. 箪：古代盛饭用的竹器。传说颜回中午吃的是早上带来的装在小竹筐里的冰冷的小米粥，吃不饱，就从井里舀一瓢水喝。"颜回井"今尚存于曲阜颜庙。

**【解读】**

本句记孔子盛赞其高徒颜回一事。颜回极贫，生活极其清苦，但他安贫乐道，刻苦学习，自我修养，不断提高自己的道德水平，与老师一道投身实践，寻求救国救民之道。

【句例】

1. 他居住在粤北山区，仅以箪食瓢饮为生，倒是健康地活到了 102 岁。

He simply lived off *very humble food and drink* in a mountainous area in north Guangdong, but managed to live healthily to the age of 102.

2. 他在纽约时曾过着箪食瓢饮的生活。后经多年奋斗，终于成为一个大公司的执行总裁。

He had once *lived an extremely poor life* in New York. After working hard for so many years, he finally became the CEO of a large company.

# 027　当仁不让

do not wait for others to go ahead when facing a just cause
do not decline to shoulder a responsibility
undoubtedly
遇到正义之事就踊跃去做，不必（对长者）谦让
承担责任而不推让
毫无疑义地

**【出处】**

子曰："当仁，不让于师。"（论语 15.36）

The Master said, "Never wait for your teacher to go ahead of you when facing a just cause."

Note: Confucius urged young people to shoulder responsibilities in upholding justice or pursuing the truth, and said that they didn't need to show modesty before their teachers in this aspect.

**【今译】**

孔子说："面对着合乎仁德的事就要坚决去做，就是在老师面前，也不必谦让。"

**【注释】**

1. 不让于师：不要等老师走在自己的前面；不必对老师谦让。

**【解读】**

日常生活中，学生后辈面对师长大多须要礼让，唯独在合乎正义的大事面前，学生后辈应随时积极力行，无须谦让，这是把道义担当摆在了第一位。孔子这一教导，是要年轻人树立社会责任感，遇事勇于担当，其社会影响非常大。现在，这句话已经简化为"当仁不让"，指遇到应该做的事就积极主动去做，义无反顾地承担责任，不要观望等待或推让。此词现在也表示"毫无疑义"，可用于褒义事例，如"他当仁不让地成为优秀模范"，也可以用于贬义事例，

如"他当仁不让地成为头号坏人"。

## 【句例】

1. 完成这项任务你是当仁不让啦。快快行动起来吧。

So you must not *wait for others to go ahead of you* in fulfilling this task. Take action and be quick.

2. 我们的向导总是当仁不让地解决我们旅途中遇到的困难。因此，他当仁不让地赢得了我们的信任。

Our guide *never declined to shoulder his responsibility* in solving the difficulties we encountered on the trip. Thus he has *undoubtedly* gained our trust.

# 028　道不同，不相为谋

Those who are not in the same camp do not plan together.
to have different idea and cannot work together
主张不同，就不要一起谋划共事。
观念不同，不能共事

【出处】

子曰："道不同，不相为谋。"（论语 15.40）

The Master said, "Those who are not in the same camp do not plan together."

Note: Confucius pointed out that people holding different views or ideals should not plan together for a goal as there was little ground for consultation or cooperation between them.

【今译】

孔子说："主张不同，就不要一起谋划共事。"

【注释】

1. 道：这里指思想观念、原则立场、学说主张、人生志向等。
2. 谋：谋划，计议，商讨，共事。

【解读】

孔子的这句话已经成了千古不易的箴言。志向不同，意见不合，是不能共谋成事的。在人与人之间相处方面，孔子提倡"和而不同"，指不同道者之间相互尊重、求同存异、和谐共处，意在强调人要有广阔的胸怀，要能包容，要有君子品格。但它跟"不相为谋"是有本质区别的。不同道者可以和而不同，你带着你的理念做你的事，我带着我的理念做我的事，大家各尽其宜。但一旦要共谋成事而意见不同，则要么争吵不断，要么妥协放弃，终归一事无成，可见不同道者是不宜相与为谋的。

【句例】

1. 道不同不相为谋，这正是两位投资者合作破裂的根本原因。

*Those who are not in the same camp do not plan together*. That is exactly the cause of the breakdown of the cooperation between the two investors.

2. 我们道不同不相为谋，最后自然是分手了。

We *had different ideas and could not work together*, so it was natural that we broke up eventually.

# 029　道听途说

to spread hearsay
rumor, hearsay
到处传播路上听到的传言
传闻、谣言

【出处】

子曰："道听而涂说，德之弃也。"（论语 17.14）

The Master said, "To spread hearsay is to betray morality."

Note: Confucius pointed out that spreading hearsay was a deviation from morality and ethics, and he denounced the eager transmitters of hearsay. He was warning people to stop spreading hearsay of a rumors.

【今译】

孔子说："到处传播路上听到的传言，这是对道德的背弃。"

【注释】

1. 涂：同"途"，道路。

【解读】

孔子指出散布传言是一种背离道德准则的行为，意在告诫人们在事实弄清之前不要轻易传播流言，更不要信谣传谣，而要做到"谣言止于智者"。

【句例】

1. 总有这么些人，他们喜欢道听途说，所以你不能指望从他们那里得到真实的信息。

There are some who just love to *spread hearsay*, so you can't rely on them to gain authentic information.

2. 关于那个城市发生恐怖袭击的新闻报道完全是道听途说，但不幸的是，它迅速传播开来。

The news report about a terrorist attack in that city was entirely *hearsay*, but unfortunately it ran apace.

# 030  发愤忘食

to forget one's meals when racking his brains without a result
to be immersed in something to forget one's meals
陷于苦思冥想而不得要领之时，连吃饭都忘了
十分专注于某事，连吃饭都忘了

【出处】

叶公问孔子于子路，子路不对。子曰："女奚不曰，其为人也，发愤忘食，乐以忘忧，不知老之将至云尔。"（论语 7.19）

Lord She asked Zilu about Confucius and got no reply. Later the Master said to Zilu, "Why not just tell him that I am no more than a man who forgets his meals when racking his brains without a result, who forgets his worries while taking delight in life, and who cares little about the increasing age?"

Note: When someone asked Zilu what Confucius was like, Zilu did not know how to answer, and Confucius suggested the above answer. He meant that he loved to learn and think and took delight in life, forgetting that he was getting old. That was Confucius' self-evaluation.

【今译】

叶公向子路问孔子是个什么样的人，子路不答。孔子（对子路）说："你为什么不这样说：他这个人呐，陷于苦思冥想而不得要领之时，他连饭都会忘记吃；而当快乐来临之时，他会把一切忧虑都抛诸脑后，就连自己快要到垂暮之年都还不知道，如此而已。"

【注释】

1. 叶公：姓沈名诸梁，字子高，楚国大夫，封地在叶城，故称叶公。叶，古音如"社"。

2. 发愤：在不得要领时极力思考。愤，苦思冥想而仍然领会不了的样子。

【解读】

当有人问子路孔子是个怎么样的人时，子路不知该如何回答，孔子就告诉

他可以作以上的应答。那也是孔子的自我评价。晚年的孔子一方面专心教学，一方面专注于古籍的整理，遇到困难或疑惑时，能刻苦钻研，积极思考，有时连饭也忘记吃。更重要的是，他把这也看作是人生的乐趣，依然在忘情地奋斗着。

【句例】

1. 那位科学家进行基因图谱研究时常常发愤忘食。

When the scientist was working on the gene map, he often *forgot his meals when racking his brains without a result*.

2. 有时候那些技校学生搞起创新项目来甚至发愤忘食。

Sometimes those technical school students were so *immersed* in their innovation project *that they even forgot their meals*.

# 031　犯而不校

to care little when offended
to forgive others for their offenses
受到别人的触犯也不计较
宽恕别人的冒犯

**【出处】**

曾子曰："以能问于不能，以多问于寡，有若无，实若虚；犯而不校——昔者吾友尝从事于斯矣。"（论语 8.5）

Zengzi said, "A talented man seeks advice from the less talented, an informed man consults the less informed, a knowledgeable man looks as if he were void of knowledge, a substantial man appears as if he were insufficient, and a man cares little when offended—such were ways in which a friend of mine used to conduct."

Note: Zengzi highly appreciated a fellow disciple of his for being modest and substantial in learning, and his forgiving others for their offenses. It is believed that he was referring to Yan Hui, who was Confucius' best disciple.

**【今译】**

曾子说："有才能的人向没有才能的人请教，知识多的人向知识少的人请教，有学问却像没学问一样；胸中很充实却好像很空虚；受人触犯也不计较——从前我的朋友就这样做过了。"

**【注释】**

1. 校：同较，即计较。

**【解读】**

曾子在这里回忆一位同学，赞扬他踏实好学、虚怀若谷、不与他人计较小事小非的高尚品格。这位同学一般被认为是颜回。

【句例】

1. 要做到犯而不校有时是很困难的，除非你有博大的胸怀。

It is difficult *to care little when you are offended* unless you are so broad-minded.

2. 我们提倡在非原则问题上的犯而不校。

We advocate *forgiving others for their offenses* on non principled issues.

# 032　犯而勿欺

better offend one face to face than deceive him covertly
offend one face to face, not deceive him covertly
犯颜直谏好于背地里欺骗
可以犯颜直谏，但不能背地里欺骗

## 【出处】

子路问事君。子曰："勿欺也，而犯之。"（论语 14.22）

When Zilu asked how to serve a state ruler, the Master said, "Better offend him face to face than deceive him covertly."

Note: Confucius pointed out that officials should not deceive their monarch but could give him explicit dissuasion even though it might mean offense to him.

## 【今译】

子路问怎样服事君主。孔子说："不能背地里欺骗他，但可以犯颜直谏。"

## 【注释】

1. 犯：冒犯，这里指犯言直谏。

## 【解读】

儒家的宗旨是忠君保民，而忠君的一大表现就是在国君施政错误时进行谏劝。然而在一些残暴的国君面前，谏劝往往意味着谏劝者的灾难，故有的大臣选择隐瞒实情，隐瞒自己的观点，甚至曲意逢迎，这是欺君祸国殃民的自私做法。孔子认为直谏虽然会冒犯国君，但总比欺骗隐瞒好。

## 【句例】

1. 犯而勿欺，才能有健康的上下级关系。

*It's better to offend one face to face than to deceive him covertly.* Only by doing this can we have sound hierarchical relationships.

2. 犯而勿欺是对待上级的正确态度。

*You may offend him face to face but must not deceive him covertly*. This is the correct attitude toward your superior.

# 033　犯上作乱

to offend the sovereign or the superior and rebel
触犯君主或上级并造反

【出处】

有子曰：“其为人也孝弟，而好犯上者，鲜矣；不好犯上，而好作乱者，未之有也。”（论语 1.2）

Youzi said, "It is a rare case that a man who has filial piety and fraternal love will be liable to offend his superior; it never occurs that a man who does not offend his superior will rebel."

Note: Confucius' disciple Youzi was reiterating his teacher's teaching on the importance of filial piety and fraternal duties. He pointed out that a filial son would not offend his superior in office or rebel against his sovereign.

【今译】

有子说：“孝顺父母，顺从兄长，而喜好触犯上级，这样的人是很少见的。不喜好触犯上级，而喜好造反的人是没有的。”

【注释】

1. 有子：孔子的弟子有若。

2. 弟：通“悌”，音 tì，敬爱兄长。

3. 上：上级，此处尤指君主。

【解读】

孔子的弟子有子重申老师关于孝悌重要性的教导。他指出，遵行孝悌的人是不会犯上作乱的。

【句例】

1. 在古代，犯上作乱那是重罪，一人犯事往往会株连整个家族。

In ancient times, *offending the sovereign and rebelling* was a felony, and the one who committed it would cause all the other family members to be implicated in it.

2. 那个军官承认犯上，但坚持说没有作乱的意图，结果还是被判处终生监禁。

The officer admitted that he *offended the superior* but insisted that he had no intention to *rebel*. Still, he was sentenced to life imprisonment as a result.

# 034  肥马轻裘

to ride in carriages drawn by well-fed horses and wear fine fur coats
to live a luxurious life
乘坐膘壮的马拉着的车子，穿着轻便暖和的皮袍
生活阔绰

## 【出处】

子曰："赤之适齐也，乘肥马，衣轻裘。吾闻之也：君子周急不济富。"（论语 6.4）

The Master said, "When Gongxi Chi is in the State of Qi, he rides in carriages drawn by well-fed horses and wears fine fur coats. I have heard that a superior man helps meet an urgent need rather than help add to the wealth of the rich. "

Note: When Gongxi Chi was sent to another state on diplomatic missions, his family could ask the government for food subsidies. However, although Gongxi Chi lived in plenty, Ran You, a majordomo of the Jisun family, gave his mother too much food allowance. Confucius criticized him because that was contrary to principle and unreasonable.

## 【今译】

孔子说："公西赤出使齐国，乘坐膘壮的马拉着的车子，穿着轻便暖和的皮袍。我听说过，君子只是救济急需的人，而不为富人增添财富。"

## 【注释】

1. 赤：公西赤，孔子的弟子，又称公西华。

2. 裘：皮衣。

3. 周急不济富：一种救济原则，即只对有紧急需要的人群实施救济，而不帮助富有的人增加财富。后世变为"救急不救穷"。

## 【解读】

当公西赤被派往他国执行外交任务时，他的家人可以向政府申请食品补贴。但是，尽管公西赤生活富足，季孙家族的管家冉有却给了他这位同门弟子

的母亲太多的食物津贴。孔子批评他，因为这是违背原则和不合理的。同时非常耐心仔细地说明反对的理由，提出一个"周急不济富"的救济原则。

【句例】

1. 奴隶主田连阡陌、肥马轻裘，从来也不会同情那些上无片瓦、衣不蔽体的奴隶。

Having possessed large amounts of fields, the slave owners *rode in carriages drawn by well-fed horses and wore fine fur coats*, and would never have sympathy on those ragged, homeless slaves.

2. 自从公司破产，杰弗逊先生便不得不告别肥马轻裘的生活。

Since the company went bankrupt, Mr. Jefferson had to bid farewell to his past *luxurious life*.

# 035　斐然成章

to have striking literary grace
with literary grace
富有文采

【出处】

子在陈曰："归与！归与！吾党之小子狂简，斐然成章，不知所以裁之。"
（论语 5.22）

When the Master was in the State of Chen, he sighed, "O I'm going home! O I'm going home! The young pupils back in my hometown are ambitious but impetuous. While having striking literary grace they still do not know how to shape themselves."

Note: When Confucius was going to end his 14 years' political tour in many other states, he declared that he would go back to his home state and focus his energy on teaching and the sorting and compiling of ancient classics. He believed that the young people back in his home state had striking literary grace but they still needed cultivating. In 484 BC, Confucius went back to his home state Lu.

【今译】

孔子在陈国说："回去哟！回去哟！家乡的弟子志向高远而处事疏阔。虽然文采可观，但还不知道怎样来裁剪节制自己。"

【注释】

1. 狂简：志向远大但行为粗率简单。
2. 斐然成章：文章富有文采，也可用来赞美一个人有文采。
3. 裁：裁剪，节制，裁正，此处指对人的品格修养进行修正完善。

【解读】

孔子 55 岁时因与季氏政见不同而离开鲁国，周游列国宣传他的治国理念，希望得到某一诸侯国君任用，辗转多国后，终因不见用而萌生归意，希望回家乡继续办学授徒和整理经典文献。他承认家乡的年轻人文采斐然，但还有待于他去培养和裁正。公元前 484 年，鲁国国卿季康子派人迎孔子归鲁。孔子周游列国 14 年至此结束。

【句例】

1. 他十六岁就能写诗为文，且斐然成章，深孚众望。

At the age of 16 he was able to write poems and articles, which *had striking literary grace* and won him great popularity.

2. 别看他其貌不扬，写起文章来却斐然成章，并因此有了大量女粉丝。

Despite his homely appearance, he writes articles *with literary grace*, and thus has a lot of female fans.

# 036　分崩离析

to fall apart　to disintegrate
崩塌解体　四分五裂

## 【出处】

子曰："今由与求也，相夫子，远人不服而不能来也，邦分崩离析而不能守也；而谋动干戈于邦内。"（论语 16.1）

The Master said, "Now, You and Qiu, assistants as you are, you have failed to help your master to win over the people who are not submissive, nor can you help prevent the state from falling apart. Instead, you are planning to resort to armed forces, even within our own territory!"

Note: Confucius severely criticized two of his disciples, Zhong You and Ran Qiu, for their failing to dissuade their greedy master, the prime minster of the State of Lu, who planned to attack and annex a city-state affiliated to their own state, and warned them that they would cause the state to fall apart. Then the two went back and reported to their master, who gave up their plan eventually.

## 【今译】

孔子说："现在，仲由和冉求你们两个人辅助季氏，远方的人不归服而不能招徕他们；国家面临分裂瓦解而不能保全，反而策划在国内使用武力。"

## 【注释】

1. 远人：指周边的少数民族。
2. 相夫子：帮助你家的主人。相，帮助，辅助。
3. 来：同"徕"，招徕，使归附，使臣服。
4. 分崩离析：崩塌解体，四分五裂。形容国家或集团分裂瓦解。

## 【解读】

周成王封东夷部落首领太皞为"颛臾王"，专门替他们祭祀蒙山。颛臾国小势弱，到了春秋初期就变成了鲁国附庸。鲁国权臣季氏为了一己之私竟想攻取它。孔子严厉批评了两位弟子，说他们身为季氏家臣而不去劝说家主放弃计划，并把不能攻取颛臾的情理对他们分析得仔细透彻，指出季氏伐颛臾实际上是一种内乱，会导致国家分崩离析。

**【句例】**

1. 一个国家若不能成功对付内忧外患，早晚是要分崩离析的。

A country would sooner or later *fall apart* if it could not manage to cope with domestic trouble and foreign invasion.

2. 要不是这位老太太接任总裁，这个公司早就分崩离析了。

If the old lady hadn't taken over as the president, the company would have *disintegrated* long before.

# 037　富贵浮云

Riches and ranks are like passing clouds.
to look upon riches and ranks as passing clouds in the sky
富贵像是天上的浮云一样。
把富贵看得像天上的浮云一样

## 【出处】

子曰："饭疏食饮水，曲肱而枕之，乐亦在其中矣。不义而富且贵，于我如浮云。"（论语 7.16）

The Master said, "Eating coarse food, drinking plain water and lying with my bended arms for a pillow are where my pleasure lies. Riches and ranks acquired by unrighteous means are to me like passing clouds."

Note: Confucius looked upon riches and ranks as something light and illusory as passing clouds in the sky. He said that instead of seeking fame and riches in an unjust way, he would rather enjoy a simple life doing freely what he wanted to do.

## 【今译】

孔子说："吃粗粮，喝清水，弯着胳膊当枕头，乐趣也就在这中间了。用不正当的手段得来的富贵，对于我来讲就像是天上的浮云一样。"

## 【注释】

1. 饭疏食：饭，作动词，是"吃"的意思。疏食即粗粮。
2. 曲肱：弯着胳膊。肱，胳膊。
3. 浮云：比喻转瞬即逝、虚而不实的东西。

## 【解读】

孔子曾说过，只要合乎原则，富贵就可以去追求，否则，他宁愿过着简朴的生活，并以此自得其乐。秉承这一原则，孔子把金钱、地位看得很轻，更把不义而得来的富贵看得像天上的浮云那样虚无缥缈、转瞬即逝。孔子视富贵如浮云，重精神轻物质，重理想轻享受，这种思想深深影响了古代的知识分子。

【句例】

1. 富贵如浮云，仁人志士是不屑一顾的。

*Riches and ranks are like passing clouds*, and a man of moral integrity would find it a scorn to take it into consideration.

2. 那位将军视富贵如浮云，断然拒绝加入反叛者的政变组织。

The general *looked upon riches and ranks as passing clouds in the sky* and absolutely refused to join the rebels in their coup group.

# 038　夫子自道

The master is referring to himself. （When the teacher speaks of others' good, he unintentionally speaks of his own similar strengths.）

老师讲的正是他自己。（当老师说到别人的优点时，他无意中说到了自己的类似优点。）

**【出处】**

子曰："君子道者三，我无能焉：仁者不忧，知者不惑，勇者不惧。"子贡曰："夫子自道也。"（论语 14.28）

The Master said, "A man of virtue should possess these three qualities, which I am still in want of: The virtuous won't be anxiety-ridden, the wise won't get bewildered and the courageous are fearless." Zigong said, "(By naming the three qualities) our master is referring to himself."

Note: Confucius emphasized three main moral qualities that a man of virtue should possess, and said modestly that he possessed none of them. But Zigong said his teacher did possess them. In ancient Chinese culture, when a man of virtue said modestly that he was in lack of some certain good qualities that he admired most, people would think that he was actually in possession of them.

**【今译】**

孔子说："君子有三个方面的品德我还未能做到：仁德的人不忧愁，聪明的人不迷惑，勇敢的人不畏惧。"子贡说："老师说的就是他自己呀。"

**【注释】**

1. 夫子自道：老师说的正是他自己。意思是，说到别人的优点，无意中却正好讲到了自己的优点。此语也有贬义用法，意思是指摘别人，无意中却正好暴露了自己同样的缺点错误。

**【解读】**

孔子论及成为一名君子必须具备的三种品质，并说他自己还没能做到。对此，学生子贡的评论是"夫子自道"。"夫子自道"的本意是，当一个人说别人好的时候，事实上正说出了自己的好，因为当他欣赏并肯定别人的优点时，他本身往往已具备同类优点。此成语也可用于贬义的事例。

【句例】

1. 林先生品德高尚。他列举前任的诸多优点，实则在许多人看来是夫子自道。

Mr. Lin has a noble character. He enumerates the many merits of his predecessor, but in many people's eyes he *is referring to himself*.

2. 讲了我们那么多不是，我看他倒是夫子自道哩。

He attributed so many defects to us, but I would rather think *he was speaking of his own* faults.

# 039　刚毅木讷

firm, resolute, simple and slow in speech
staunch, resolute, plain and cautious in speech
刚强、果敢、质朴、慎言

【出处】

子曰："刚、毅、木、讷近仁。"（论语 13.27）

The Master said, "Being firm, resolute, simple and slow in speech is close to benevolence."

Note: Confucius listed the four virtues that a man should possess on his way to benevolence. "Benevolence" is a special term that represents the highest moral standard and the highest level of thought in ancient China. Confucius believed that if one possessed those four virtues, he was close to being benevolence.

【今译】

孔子说："刚强、果敢、质朴、慎言，这四种品德接近于仁。"

【注释】

1. 木：质朴。

2. 讷：原指说话迟钝，这里指言语谨慎。

【解读】

孔子列举了一个人在通往仁道的道路上应该具备的四种美德。"仁"是中国古代代表最高道德标准和最高思想水平的专用名词。孔子认为，如果一个人拥有他说过的那四种美德，他就接近于仁。

【句例】

1. 刚毅木讷是个好品质，既可以增强一个人的执行力，又可以让他说话谨慎。

*Being firm, resolute, simple and slow in speech* is a fine quality. It can not only help a person enhance his execution power, but also make him cautious in speech.

2. 他为人刚毅木讷，许多人认为他值得深交。

He is *staunch, resolute, plain and cautious in speech*, and many people think he is worth a deep friendship.

# 040 割鸡用牛刀

to kill a chicken with an ox-cleaver
to break a butterfly on the wheel
杀鸡用宰牛的刀
花大气力去办小事情

**【出处】**

子之武城，闻弦歌之声。夫子莞尔而笑，曰："割鸡焉用牛刀？"（论语 17.4）

When the Master visited Wucheng and heard songs sung to the stringed instruments, he smiled at it, saying, "Why kill a chicken with an ox-cleaver?"

Note: Confucius had always attached great importance to the educational function of proprieties and music, and Yan Yan carried out the education in Wucheng with great achievements. Confucius might think that there was no need to play elegant music in a small place like Wucheng, so he laughed at Yan Yan (Ziyou) , saying that he was killing a chicken with an ox-cleaver. After Yan Yan corrected him, he realized that he had made a slip of the tongue, and said that he was joking. In this way he admitted his mistake skillfully, and at the same time saved his face.

**【今译】**

孔子到武城，听见弹琴唱歌的声音。孔子笑了笑，说："杀鸡何必用宰牛的刀呢？"

**【注释】**

1. 武城：鲁国的一个小城，当时子游（言偃）是武城的行政长官。

2. 弦歌：以琴瑟伴奏歌唱。弦，指琴瑟。弦歌是子游以礼乐治邑的做法之一，是对老师教诲的实践。

**【解读】**

孔子一向重视礼乐的教化作用，而言偃正是秉承老师的教导在武城实施礼乐教化并成果斐然。孔子可能因为脑子里想的尽是些治国平天下的大事，竟觉得小地方无须演唱高雅的乐曲，所以才嘲笑言偃（子游）是"杀鸡用牛刀"，待言偃指正后，方知自己失言，只好推说是开个玩笑，巧妙地承认了错误，还保住了面子。

【句例】

1. 割鸡焉用牛刀。叫个低级官员去处理一下就行了。

No need to *kill a chicken with an ox-cleaver*. It's all right to let a lower officer go and deal with it.

2. 让好几位医生会诊来为他治感冒，这不是割鸡用牛刀吗？

Several doctors were consulted to treat his cold! Isn't it to *break a butterfly on the wheel*?

# 041 功亏一篑

to fail to pile up a mound for lack of one basket of earth
to miss the mark by a narrow margin
只缺一筐土而不能完成造山任务
做事情只差最后一步而没能完成

## 【出处】

子曰："譬如为山，未成一篑，止，吾止也；譬如平地，虽覆一篑，进，吾往也。（论语 9.19）

The Master said, "Let's take piling up earth to make a mound for example. When I need only one basket of earth to complete the whole work but I stop, it is none other than I who have made the stop. Again let's take the leveling up of land for example. I may add only one basket of earth. It is a step forward and it is none other than I who have taken that step."

Note: According to Confucius, one should have perseverance in doing anything, and if he gives up a thing when it is nearly completed, it would mean total failure, and he himself is to blame for it.

## 【今译】

孔子说："譬如用土堆山，只差一筐土就完成了，这时停下来，那是我自己要停下来的；譬如在平整土地，虽然只倒下一筐，这就把工作推进了一步，而那是我自己推进的。"

## 【注释】

1. 未成一篑：因少挑一筐土而没能完成堆山的任务，比喻做事情半途而废、功亏一篑。篑，土筐。

2. 吾往也：是我自己做的。

## 【解读】

按孔子的说法，一个人做任何事情都应该持之以恒，如果他在一件事情快要完成时放弃了它，这将意味着彻底的失败，他自己应该为此负责。

【句例】

1. 你拒绝写论文而失去获得博士学位的机会，在我看来是功亏一篑啊。

You refused to write a dissertation and lost the opportunity to earn a doctoral degree. It seems to me like you have *failed to pile up a mound for lack of one basket of earth.*

2. 你为什么不继续写你的小说呢？功亏一篑，你不觉得可惜吗？

Why don't you continue to write your fiction? Don't you think it a pity to have *missed the mark by a narrow margin*?

# 042　工欲善其事，必先利其器

A workman must sharpen his tools if he is to do his work well.
A workman must sharpen his tools for better work
工匠想把活儿做好，必须首先磨利他的工具。
工匠先把工具磨利，才能把活儿做好

**【出处】**

子贡问为仁。子曰："工欲善其事，必先利其器。居是邦也，事其大夫之贤者，友其士之仁者。"（论语 15.10）

When Zigong asked how to practice benevolence, the Master said, "If a workman wishes to do his job well, he must first sharpen his tools. So when you stay in a state, try to associate with the virtuous high officials, and make friends with the virtuous scholars."

Note: Confucius used a metaphor to tell Zigong that in order to accomplish something great in another state, he should first try to contact the virtuous high-ranking officials and scholars there. To implement a notion of state administration, it is necessary to have the approval of the monarch, but gaining the support from the officials around him in advance is just like to sharpen the tools before a carpenter starts work, and the possibility of success is of course greater. In reality, Zigong did what Confucius taught him to do, and became an outstanding diplomat.

**【今译】**

子贡问怎样做到仁。孔子说："工匠想把活儿做好，必须首先磨利他的工具。你住在这个国家，就要服事大夫中的那些贤者，结交士人中的仁者。"

**【注释】**

1. 善其事：把事情做好，此处指做出好的木作。
2. 利其器：把他的工具磨快。

**【解读】**

子贡问如何实践仁，孔子根据他口才好、外交能力强、有正义感、有资财、能成大事等特点，为他指出"结交各国贤大夫和仁人志士"的具体方法。一个治国理念要得以实施，须有国君的认可，但事先做好他周围贤大夫的工作，那无异于木匠开工之前先磨好工具，成事的可能性当然更大。子贡最终没有辜负老师的厚望，在各国广交贤明，故而处理外交事务左右逢源，游刃有余，为鲁国的国家安全和利益做出了很大的贡献。

【句例】

1. 工欲善其事，必先利其器，所以基础工作必须预先做好。

*A workman must sharpen his tools if he is to do his work well*, so basic work must be done in advance.

2. 工欲善其事，必先利其器。想要成功，我们就必须有充分的准备。

Just as *a workman must sharpen his tools for better work*, we should make full preparations for success.

# 043  怪力乱神

weird things, supernatural powers, riots
and spiritual beings,
weird stuffs
怪异之事、超自然力、暴动变乱、鬼神
怪事

**【出处】**

子不语怪、力、乱、神。（论语 7.21）

The Master would not talk of weird things, supernatural powers, riots or spiritual beings.

Note: One of the greatest characteristics of early Confucianism was that they didn't believed in the supernatural beings. They focused mainly on human affairs and objected to riots and other extreme actions.

**【今译】**

孔子不谈论怪异之事、超自然力、暴动变乱、鬼神。

**【注释】**

1. 怪：妖或精一类的奇异神秘之物；怪异反常的现象。
2. 力：超自然力，如巫祝消灾祈福、神仙显灵作法等。
3. 乱：暴乱，变乱，叛乱，悖乱（如子臣弑杀父君）。

**【解读】**

早期儒家最大的特点之一就是他们不相信超自然的存在。他们的主要关注是人事而非鬼神，并反对暴乱和其他极端行为。

**【句例】**

1. 这些小说专讲怪、力、乱、神等乱七八糟的东西，竟然还能畅销，岂非咄咄怪事？！

Isn't it strange that such novels should sell well which bear rubbish like *weird things, supernatural powers, riots or spiritual beings*?!

2. 别在这里跟我们讲怪、力、乱、神。这里是科学讲坛。

No *weird stuffs* for us here. This is the science forum.

# 044　过犹不及

Going beyond is as wrong as falling short.
Going too far is as bad as not going far enough.
事情做得过头，就跟做得不够一样，都是不好的。

## 【出处】

子贡问："师与商也孰贤？"子曰："师也过，商也不及。"曰："然则师愈与？"子曰："过犹不及。"（论语 11.16）

When Zigong asked which was better, Zhuansun Shi or Bu Shang, the Master said, "Shi often goes beyond, while Shang still falls short."

"Then may I say Shi is better?" asked Zigong.

"No. Going beyond is as wrong as falling short," replied the Master.

Note: Confucius evaluated two of his disciples, saying that neither of them was good enough because they were either too radical or too conservative. Confucius believed that the doctrine of the mean (the Golden Mean) was the best policy for one's actions and thought.

## 【今译】

子贡问孔子："颛孙师和卜商二人谁更好一些呢？"孔子回答说："子张做事常常过头，子夏常常做得不够。"子贡说："那么是子张好一些吗？"孔子说："不对。事情事情做得过头，就跟做得不够一样，都是不好的。"

## 【注释】

1. 师与商：颛孙师和卜商。即子张和子夏。

2. 愈：胜过，强些。

3. 过犹不及：事情做过头跟做得不够同样不合适。

## 【解读】

孔子认为子张偏激而子夏保守，希望他的学生不走极端，弥补各自的不足。这是孔子中庸哲学思想的体现。

【句例】

1. 给任何花草浇水都得有个度。过犹不及，这道理适用于任何事物。

Proper amounts of water should be given to any flowers and grass. *Going beyond is as wrong as falling short*. This principle can be applied to all things.

2. 过犹不及。看来你得少给你的学生布置作业啦。

*Going too far is as bad as not going far enough*. It seems that you should not assign too much homework to your students.

# 045  过则勿惮改

Don't be afraid to correct mistakes.
Don't hesitate to correct mistakes.
有了过错，就不要怕改正

## 【出处】

子曰："君子不重则不威；学则不固。主忠信。无友不如己者；过则勿惮改。"（论语 1.8）

The Master said, "Without a stately manner a superior man cannot stand on dignity, nor can he lay a solid learning foundation. He should hold the sense of loyalty and faithfulness as prime principle, and have no friends of lower levels. When he has faults, he should not be afraid to correct them."

Note: Confucius pointed out that a man in a position of dominance should show a dignified manner, have a good personality and be prepared to correct his mistakes.

## 【今译】

孔子说："君子不庄重就没有威严，所学知识也不能牢固。要把忠信当成做人的首要原则，不要跟不如自己的人交往；有了过错，就不要怕改正。"

## 【注释】

1. 惮：害怕。

## 【解读】

孔子认为负有领导职责的君子和具有理想人格的君子，除了质朴的内在品质之外，从外表上还应当给人以庄重大方、威严深沉的形象，使人感到稳重可靠，能付以重托。他们应该多与价值观相同的人相处交往。有了错误，要敢于承认，不要害怕因此而有损自己的威严。实际上，君子承认并改正错误，定能得到更多的拥戴。

**【句例】**

1. 过则勿惮改，这样你就能得到更多人的信任和拥护。

When you have faults, *don't be afraid to correct them*. Thus you will gain more trust and support.

2. 领导机构跟个人一样，过则勿惮改，这样既可以减少施政错误，又不损领导权威。

A governing body, like an individual, *should not hesitate to correct mistakes*. This can reduce the policy errors without the loss of authority.

# 046　和而不同

to harmonize without demanding conformity
to harmonize without following blindly
和谐相处而不强求一致
和谐相处而不盲目附和

## 【出处】

子曰："君子和而不同，小人同而不和。"（论语 13.23）

The Master said, "The superior men harmonize without demanding conformity; the base men demand conformity but do not harmonize."

Note: According to Confucius, the virtuous people would seek harmony in their association while allowing each individual to have different thought or view points. Thus they might reach agreements by coordinating different opinions but didn't impose one's idea upon the other. On the other hand, the virtueless people would clique by mingling up different opinions while scheming against each other for their selfish benefits.

## 【今译】

孔子说："君子和谐相处而不强求一致，小人强求一致而不和谐相处。"

## 【注释】

1. 和：指在人际交往中通过求同存异与他人保持一种和谐友善的关系，但在对具体问题的看法上却不必苟同于对方。

2. 同：强求一致，盲目附从，是一种无原则的、表面附和的人际关系。

## 【解读】

"和而不同"是孔子思想体系中的重要组成部分。"和"是一个非常重要的概念，指的是一种有差别的、多样性的统一。"和而不同"，是一种有原则的和谐的人际关系。君子可以与他周围的人保持和谐融洽的关系，但对待任何事情都能独立思考，不强求一致，不盲目附和。"同而不和"，是指在对问题的看法上迎合别人的心理、附和别人的言论，但在内心深处却并不抱和谐友善的态度，不能与人保持融洽友好的关系。

【句例】

1. 我们这么大的一个单位，只有做到和而不同才有力量应对复杂的外部环境。

Ours is a large organization. Only by *harmonizing without demanding conformity* can we cope with the complex external environment.

2. 和而不同就会有真团结。同而不和则是表面一团和气而内部勾心斗角。

We shall have genuine solidarity when we *harmonize without following blindly*. Following blindly without harmonizing will mean superficial uniformity and internal strife.

# 047　后生可畏

Young people are a worthy challenge.
Young people should be regarded with respect.
年轻人值得敬畏。
年轻人值得尊重。

## 【出处】

子曰："后生可畏，焉知来者之不如今也？四十、五十而无闻焉，斯亦不足畏也已。"（论语 9.23）

The Master said, "Young people are a worthy challenge. Who says that the younger generation will not be as good as the older?

"But those who still haven't made their mark in their forties or fifties will deserve no reverence."

Note: Confucius warned the older people that the younger generation might surpass them. Meanwhile, he warned the young people not to idle away their prime years lest they should accomplish nothing when old.

## 【今译】

孔子说："年轻人是值得敬畏的，怎么就知道后一代不如前一代呢？但是如果到了四五十岁时还默默无闻，那他就没有什么可以敬畏的了。"

## 【注释】

1. 可畏：值得敬畏。
2. 无闻：无闻于世，不出名。

## 【解读】

这是孔子对年轻人的赞誉和期待。年轻是一种财富，就这点就值得人羡慕敬重，但年轻人又是一种挑战，上一辈一不小心就会被超越，故又值得畏惧。同时，孔子对年轻人发出鞭策，希望他们不会因为虚度青春而到老还默默无闻。

**【句例】**

1. 真是后生可畏。再不努力我们这一代人就要落伍了。

It's true that *young people are a worthy challenge*. If we go on this way without working hard, this generation of ours will fall behind.

2. 后生可畏，不出几年这些年轻人就会超过我们所有的人。

*Young people should be regarded with respect*. In just a few years they will surpass all of us.

# 048 患得患失

to worry about personal gains and losses
to focus only on personal gains and losses
担心个人的得和失
斤斤计较个人得失

**【出处】**

子曰："鄙夫可与事君也与哉？其未得之也，患得之。既得之，患失之。苟患失之，无所不至矣。"（论语 17.15）

The Master said, "Can we serve the prince together with those mean fellows?

"Before gaining official posts they worry that they might not gain them. After gaining them they worry that they might lose them again. For fear that they might lose their positions they would resort to any possible tricks to grip them."

Note: Some officials worried only about their own positions and interests, and resorted to all evil means to acquire and keep them. Confucius warned against working with such immoral officials.

**【今译】**

孔子说："可以和一个卑劣的家伙一起服事君主吗？他在没有得到官位时，总担心得不到官位。已经得到了官位，又怕失去它。一旦担心失掉官位，那他就什么事都干得出来了。"

**【注释】**

1. 鄙夫：郊野及边远之地称"边鄙"，故"鄙夫"指乡下人。品质粗俗也称"鄙"，故"鄙夫"也指人品鄙陋的人。本句中指后者。

2. 患：忧患，担心。

**【解读】**

孔子批评了当时一些在朝为官的人，他们一心贪求功名利禄，尚未得到时唯恐得不到，故不择手段以求之；得到后又唯恐失去，便无所不用其极想保住。这种人是不可能想到为国为民谋福祉的，也是不值得与其共处一朝的。

【句例】

1. 一个人如果患得患失，那就很难有一种平和的心态来追求事业的成功。

If one *worries only about his personal gains and losses*, it will be difficult for him to have a peaceful mindset to pursue success in his career.

2. 你要多想想当官能为国家人民做些什么，不要在职务升迁问题上患得患失。

You should think more about what you can do for the country and people. Never *focus only on your personal gains or losses* in job promotion.

# 049　诲人不倦　学而不厌

to teach without weariness
never feel tired of giving instructions
教书育人不知疲倦
（见 144）

【出处】

子曰："默而识之，学而不厌，诲人不倦，何有于我哉？"（论语 7.2）

The Master said, "Learning by heart and bearing in mind what is learned, studying without satiety and teaching without weariness — what difficulty is there for me to do so?"

Note: Confucius introduced an important studying method and told about his attitude toward learning and teaching. In all his teaching career, Confucius truly gave his disciples instructions without feeling weary.

【今译】

孔子说："默默记住所学知识，学习从不满足，教书育人不知疲倦，这些对我来说有什么难呢？"

【注释】

1. 识：同"志"，"记住"的意思。

2. 厌：繁体字同"饜"，原意为饱食，这里指满足。不厌即不满足、不自满。

3. 何有：何难之有。

【解读】

孔子介绍了一种重要的学习方法，并阐述了他对学习和教学的态度。在孔子的整个教学生涯中，他真正做到了对弟子言传身教而不疲。

【句例】

1. 学而不厌，诲人不倦，这是我们老师应有的态度。

The attitude that we teachers should have is *to learn without satiety and teach without weariness*.

2. 王主任一向诲人不倦，我们公司的年轻人受益匪浅。

Director Wang has *never felt tired of giving instructions*, from which the young people in our company have benefited greatly.

# 050　惠而不费

to render others benefits at little of one's own expense
to pay lip service only (irony)
给人以实惠而自己却无所耗费
口惠而实不至（讽刺用法）

## 【出处】

子曰："君子惠而不费，劳而不怨，欲而不贪，泰而不骄，威而不猛。"（论语 20.2）

The Master said, "A superior man should render benefits at little of his expense, employ the people without causing complaints, pursue what he desires without being greedy, maintain a dignified ease without looking arrogant, and look majestic without being fierce,"

Note: Confucius introduced a policy that would benefit the people substantially: The government allowed and encouraged the people to do things that would best benefit themselves without having to consume the state resources. It also means helping others without spending your own money.

## 【今译】

孔子说："主政者要给百姓以实惠而自己却无所耗费；动用百姓劳作而又不使他们心生怨恨；有所追求但不贪图财利；庄重而不傲慢；威严而不凶猛。"

## 【注释】

1. 惠而不费：给别人好处而自己却无所耗费。惠，恩惠，好处；费，花费。后世偶然也指口头上帮助人而行动上却没做到。

2. 泰：庄重。

## 【解读】

惠而不费是古代统治阶级一种开明的统治方法。它给民众带来利益却不用耗费国家钱财。具体运作中，统治阶级要"因民之所利而利之"，即实施正确的政策，因势利导，与民方便，鼓励民众自力更生勤劳致富，与此同时政府可以少投入甚至不必投入。此句也讲帮助他人而不用耗费自己的钱财。

【句例】

1. 因势利导，助民致富，这种惠而不费的政策应该大加提倡。

Making the best of the situation to guide the people in getting rich is a policy that should be advocated as it will *render benefits at little of the government's expense*.

2. 讲好了要给我们三十万美元贷款，至今却不见一分钱。该不是惠而不费吧。

They've promised a loan of three hundred thousand US dollars, but we still don't see a penny yet. I wish they wouldn't be *paying lip service only*.

# 051　祸起萧墙

to suffer from the trouble inside one's own house
Trouble arises within one's own door.
to start a civil strife
*祸乱发生在家里*
*内部发生祸乱*

**【出处】**

子曰："吾恐季孙之忧，不在颛臾，而在萧墙之内也。"（论语 16.1）

The Master said, "I am afraid that before he suffers from the possible trouble from Zhuanyu, your master Jisun would have to suffer from the trouble inside his own palace!"

Note: The Jisun Family, a royal family that controlled the power of the State of Lu, tried to attack and annex Zhuanyu, a city-state affiliated to Lu. Confucius severely criticized two of his disciples for their failing to dissuade their greedy master from doing it, and warned them of the danger of a civil strife.

**【今译】**

孔子说："我只怕季孙的忧患不在颛臾，而是在自己内部呢！"

**【注释】**

1. 颛臾：春秋时期鲁国的附庸，专门替周天子负责祭祀蒙山。

2. 萧墙之内：指祸乱缘起于内部。萧墙即屏风墙，是古代人面对大门起屏障作用的矮墙，用于遮挡视线，防止外人向内窥视。

**【解读】**

季孙氏不但把持鲁国朝政，而且试图并吞作为鲁国附庸国的颛臾以自肥。子路和冉有当时为季氏家臣，不能劝阻主人，受到孔子的严厉批评。孔子指出这样做必然引起鲁国的内乱。

【句例】

1. 再不赶快处理好公司内部各种矛盾，恐怕不久就要祸起萧墙了。

If all sorts of inconsistency are not properly dealt with in time, I'm afraid we'll *suffer from the trouble inside* our company.

2. 那个国家疯狂对外侵略扩张，引起国内各种矛盾集中爆发，很快就祸起萧墙了。

That country was crazy about aggression and expansion abroad, and had triggered all kinds of domestic conflicting, which soon *started the civil strife*.

# 052　己所不欲，勿施于人

Never impose on others what you would not choose for yourself.
Do not do to others what you don't want others to do to you.
自己不想要的，不要强加给别人。

**【出处】**

子贡问曰："有一言而可以终身行之者乎？"子曰："其恕乎！己所不欲，勿施于人。"（论语 15.24）

Zigong asked his teacher, "Is there one single word that we can practice all our life?"

The Master said, "It must be 'reciprocity'! Never impose on others what you would not choose for yourself."

Note: Confucius put forth the philosophy of reciprocity as one of his most important guidelines in dealing with interpersonal relationship. The Confucians believe that men share similar likes and dislikes, so when we want to do something to others, we should first ask ourselves whether we would like others to do the same thing to us. The philosophy of reciprocity has helped make Confucius one of the greatest social philosophers in the world.

**【今译】**

子贡问孔子问道："有没有一个字可以终身奉行的呢？"孔子回答说："那就是恕吧！自己不想要的，不要强加给别人。"

**【注释】**

1. 恕：站在别人的位置上设身处地地为别人着想，自己不想要的，不要强加给别人。恕属于儒家哲学范畴，又称"恕道"。

**【解读】**

儒家认为人有着相似的好恶，所以当我们想要对别人做某一件事情时，首先要问自己是否愿意别人对你做同样的事。这就是"己所不欲，勿施于人"，是儒家的恕道。孔子把恕道作为他处理人际关系的最重要的准则之一，这一点也使他成为世界上最伟大的哲学家之一。

【句例】

1. 己所不欲，勿施于人，这一儒家恕道要求我们要能设身处地地为他人着想。

*Never impose on others what you would not choose for yourself.* This Confucian philosophy of reciprocity requires us to place ourselves in other people's position and be considerate of them.

2. 己所不欲，勿施于人，你自己不喝酒，就别再强迫我喝酒了吧。

*Do not do to others what you don't want others to do to you.* Since you won't drink, will you please not have me drink any more?

# 053   既来之，则安之

Since they have been won round, we should try to appease them.
Now that you have come, enjoy your stay here.
take things as they come

既然把他们招来了，就要把他们安顿下来。（原意，今少用。）

既然来了，就要安下心来。（后世误读，今多用。）

既然遇到这样的事，那就静心对待吧。（同上）

【出处】

子曰："夫如是，故远人不服，则修文德以来之。既来之，则安之。"（论语 16.1）

The Master said, "After all these goals are achieved, if the people in outlying areas are still not submissive, we should win them over with our civilization, and when they have been won round, we should try to appease them.

Note: Confucius severely criticized two of his disciples, Zhong You and Ran Qiu, for their failing to dissuade their greedy master, Prime Minster Jisun of the State of Lu, who tried to attack and annex a city-state affiliated to their own state, and told them that the best policy was to win over the minorities there and let them settle down happily in the state. In this way he had the Jisun Family give up their attempt.

【今译】

孔子说："如果这样做了，边远的人民还不归服，便提倡文明道德招徕他们；已经归服了，就安抚他们。"

【注释】

1. 来：招徕。指对少数民族的招抚。

【解读】

鲁国权臣季氏为了一己之私想攻取鲁国附庸国颛臾。孔子除了批评两位弟子作为季氏的家臣不能制止季氏行为外，还给他们指出正确的做法，就是对少数民族实行安抚政策。这样，原本季氏所谓颛臾人会对他们构成威胁的借口便不能成立。最终，孔子打消了季氏并吞颛臾的企图。

【句例】

　　1. 既来之，则安之。来了就多住几天吧。

*Now that you have come, enjoy your stay here* for a few more days.

　　2. 既来之，则安之，心里不要着急。你的病会慢慢好起来的。

*Take things as they come since you are ill.* You will recover step by step.

# 054　既往不咎

Let bygones be bygones.
to overlook one's past errors
过去了的事就不必再追究了。

【出处】

　　哀公问社于宰我，宰我对曰："夏后氏以松，殷人以柏，周人以栗，曰：使民战栗。"子闻之，曰："成事不说，遂事不谏，既往不咎。"（论语 3.21）

Prince Ai asked Zai Wo about (what wood should be used in making a spirit tablet for) the altar for God of Land.

"In the Xia Dynasty, pine was used; in Yin, cypress; in Zhou, chestnut," replied Zai Wo. Then he added "Chestnut was meant to cause the people to shudder."

When Confucius heard the remark, he said, "Don't mention things already done. No dissuasion for a past wrong-doing. Let bygones be bygones."

Note: Confucius' disciple Zai Wo said that kings of the Zhou Dynasty used chestnut wood to cause the people to shudder when making a spirit tablet for the altar for God of Land. "Chestnut" sounds like "shudder" in Chinese. Confucius said that Zai Wo was talking nonsense, but he chose to pass the matter by.

【今译】

　　鲁哀公问宰我，土地神的神主牌应该用什么木头来制作，宰我回答："夏朝用松木，商朝用柏木，周朝用栗木。"又说："用栗木的意思是要使老百姓战栗。"孔子听到后说："已经做过的事不用提了，已经做过的事不用再去劝阻了，过去了的事就不必再追究了。"

【注释】

　　1. 社：土神庙，这里指土地神。

　　2. 宰我：姓宰名予，字子我。善言辞，孔子弟子。

　　3. 夏后氏：即"夏代"。夏朝君主以夏后为氏，这里以氏借指夏朝。

4. 战栗：发抖。宰我说周朝用栗木做神主牌是为了让老百姓害怕、发抖，实为荒诞。

## 【解读】

此句记孔子弟子宰我对各朝代神主牌用木的议论。宰我认为周朝统治者用栗木做神主牌是为了让民众战栗，实在是望文生义。社主牌用材因时因地而异，当无政治含义。孔子明显不同意宰我的说法，也告诫他今后说话要小心，但不加以追究。

## 【句例】

1. 我们的态度是既往不咎。

Our attitude is one of *letting bygones be bygones.*

2. 重要的是，你得学会宽恕，对她既往不咎。

What is important is that you should learn to forgive her and *overlook her past errors.*

# 055  见利思义

to check if it is righteous before a chance of gain
to think about what is right at the sight of profit
面对获利机会要考虑是否符合义理

**【出处】**

子曰:"见利思义,见危授命,久要不忘平生之言,亦可以为成人矣。"(论语 14.12)

"He can be counted as a perfect man all the same if he can check if it is righteous before a chance of gain, if he is ready to give his life at the critical moment, and if he won't forget his life-long promise even when trapped in long-standing poverty."

Note: Confucius listed the three merits that he believed might help one to become a person of perfect personality. To check if it is righteous before a chance of gain reflects Confucius' correct thought in dealing with moral principles and material interests.

**【今译】**

孔子说:"面对获利机会要考虑是否符合义理,生死关头能勇于献身,久受窘困还不忘一生的重大承诺,这样也可以成为一位完美的人。"

**【注释】**

1. 久要:长期处于穷困中。要,音 yāo,意同"约",贫困、窘困。

2. 成人:完美的人。

**【解读】**

孔子列举出他认为可以帮助一个人成为完美人格的三个优点。"见利思义"反映了孔子在处理道德原则和物质利益方面的正确思想。

**【句例】**

1. 只有见利思义,才能在面对诱惑时保持廉洁自律。

One must *check if it is righteous before a chance of gain* before he can be clean-handed and self-disciplined when facing temptation.

2. 在物欲泛滥的年代，能做到见利思义的人已经不多了。

In the age of materialism, there are few people who will *think about what is right at the sight of profit.*

# 056 见危授命

to give life at the critical moment
to die for ... in time of danger
生死关头能勇于献身
危急时刻勇于牺牲

【出处】

子曰："见利思义，见危授命，久要不忘平生之言，亦可以为成人矣。"（论语 14.12）

"He can be counted as a perfect man all the same if he can check if it is righteous before a chance of gain, if he is ready to give his life at the critical moment, and if he won't forget his life-long promise even when trapped in long-standing poverty."

Note: Confucius listed the three merits that he believed might help one to become a person of perfect personality. To be ready to give life at the critical moment reflects the sense of social responsibility and national responsibility advocated by the Confucian school.

【今译】

孔子说："面对获利机会要考虑是否符合义理，生死关头能勇于献身，久受窘困还不忘一生的重大承诺，这样也可以成为一位完美的人。"

【注释】

1. 授命：献出生命，为……而牺牲。
2. 成人：完美的人。

【解读】

孔子提出见利思义、见危授命、久要不忘平生之言作为"成人"的三个标准。见危授命反映了儒家所提倡的社会责任感和民族责任感。

【句例】

1. 见危授命也是一个人的勇敢和正义感的体现。

To be ready to *give life at the critical moment* also reflects a man's bravery and his sense of justice.

2. 国难当头，我相信很多人是愿意见危授命的。

I believe that many people would be ready to *die for* our country *in time of* national crisis.

# 057　见贤思齐

When you meet a virtuous man, try to become his equal.
to hope to learn from those who are better than oneself
to hope to learn from a role model
见到贤明人，就应该想向他看齐。
希望向那些具有优良品质的人学习
希望向模范人物学习

【出处】

子曰："见贤思齐焉，见不贤而内自省也。"（论语 4.17）

The Master said, "When you meet a virtuous man, try to become his equal; when you see something bad in others, try to engage in introspection."

Note: Confucius pointed out that one should try to emulate the virtuous people to do good, and tried to avoid errors that the virtueless people might commit.

【今译】

孔子说："见到贤明人，就应该想向他看齐；见到不贤的人，就应该自我反省。"

【注释】

1. 思齐：想向人看齐。齐，等同，一致。
2. 内自省：内心自我反省。

【解读】

此句讲人的自我修养机会无处不在，只要有心，则无论见贤、见不贤，都能找到值得自己学习和借鉴的机会。

【句例】

1. 要做到见贤思齐，只有这样你才能不断提高自己的思想品质和能力。

*When you meet a virtuous person, try to become his equal.* Only in this way can you keep improving your moral quality and working ability.

2. 他的事迹一经传开，他便成为青少年见贤思齐的榜样。

Once his story spread, he became *a role model* that teenagers *hoped to learn from*.

# 058　见义勇为

to take action at the critical moment
to fight bravely at the critical moment
关键时刻挺身而出

**【出处】**

子曰："见义不为，无勇也。"（论语 2.24）

The Master said, "Failing to take action at the critical moment shows a lack of courage."

Note: Confucius encouraged people to take action at the critical moment.

**【今译】**

孔子说："关键时刻不能挺身而出，那是怯懦。"

**【注释】**

1. 义：古注"义者，宜也"，指事情要适合做才去做，现指行为要符合义理。

**【解读】**

孔子并没有提出过"见义勇为"的说法，但他说的"见义不为无勇"恰恰反衬"见义勇为"的必要性，所以说孔子提倡见义勇为从本质上来说是没有错的。现在，见义勇为多指关键时刻为伸张正义而冒生命危险与坏人搏斗。

**【句例】**

1. 如果我们要求更多的人见义勇为，那就要确保这些勇敢的人们在行动中受到伤害时能得到公平的对待。

If we require more people to *take action at the critical moment*, we should make sure that such brave people are fairly treated when they get injured in the action.

2. 那位年轻人见义勇为，在与劫匪搏斗的过程中献出了自己的生命。

*At the critical moment* the young man *fought* against the robbers *bravely* and gave his life.

# 059  尽善尽美

perfectly good and perfectly beautiful
to have achieved the acme of perfection
极其完善，极其美好
达到完美的极点

## 【出处】

子谓韶："尽美矣，又尽善也；"谓武："尽美矣，未尽善也。(论语 3.25)

The Master evaluated the music *Shao*, saying, "It is perfectly beautiful, and perfectly good." Then to the music *Wu* he said, "it is perfectly beautiful, but not perfectly good."

Note: Confucius evaluated two kinds of music by distinguishing their formats and nature. The music *Shao* was in a peaceful melody about the ancient Chinese sage king Shun who peacefully succeeded to the throne from his predecessor Yao. The music *Wu* was in a militant tune about King Wu who resorted to armed forces in overthrowing the previous dynasty. Confucius loved the former for its peaceful melody as he was tired of the turmoil in his time. Thus he said that the music *Shao* was perfectly good and perfectly beautiful.

## 【今译】

孔子讲到《韶》这一乐曲时说："艺术形式美极了，内容也很好。"谈到《武》这一乐曲时说："艺术形式很美，但内容却还达不到完美的程度。"

## 【注释】

1. 韶：相传是古代歌颂舜的一种乐舞。
2. 武：相传是歌颂周武王伐纣事迹的乐舞。

## 【解读】

此句记孔子对当时流行的两种正乐的评价。后世学者认为《韶》歌颂的是尧对舜禅位的平和的政权过渡，其乐舞优美且情操高尚，所以孔子才会认为它尽美而尽善，而《武》乐虽雄壮优美，但本身有杀伐之气，故曰尽美而未尽善。音乐有陶冶情性、和融社会的功用，必须符合"中和"的原则。这里讲的《武》

乐不尽善，是指它不够"中和"，即不够中正平和。

【句例】

1. 虽然这幅油画并不尽善尽美，但画家已经是尽力而为了。

Although this oil painting is not *perfectly good or perfectly beautiful*, the artist has done it to the best of his ability.

2. 刘先生练习中国书法已经三十多年了，现在他在这方面已经达到了尽善尽美的境界。

Mr. Liu has practiced Chinese calligraphy for over thirty years, and now he *has achieved the acme of perfection* in this sphere.

# 060 敬而远之

to keep aloof from … while showing respect to…
to shun somebody or something
对……表示尊敬却不愿接近
避开某人或某事物

## 【出处】

樊迟问知，子曰："务民之义，敬鬼神而远之，可谓知矣。"（论语 6.22）

When Fan Chi asked what wisdom was, the Master said, "Focus on what ought to be done for the people and keep aloof from ghosts and deities while showing respect to them. That could be called wisdom."

Note: Confucius told his disciple Fan Chi to pay enough respect to the supernatural beings, because in a world full of their worshipers it might help win the people's support , but he also warned him not to go too far into it. Instead, he told him to focus on the substantial work for the people. This shows the humanistic nature of the Confucianism.

## 【今译】

樊迟问孔子怎样才算是智，孔子说："专心做好该为老百姓做的事，尊敬鬼神但不要过分亲近它们，这就可以说是智了。"

## 【注释】

1. 知：同"智"。
2. 务：从事、致力于。
3. 义：合宜、合理的事，该做的事。

## 【解读】

本句虽然只是孔子对一位学生问知（智）的解答，却留下了"务民之义，敬鬼神而远之"的千古名言，给儒家思想打上了"尽人事"的烙印。所谓尽人事，就是关系到人的实事做好，而不在鬼神这些虚无的东西上过多地浪费时间和精力。鬼是祖先，敬祖先是孝道的延续；神有天神地祇，祭神是对天地神祇的敬畏。祭祀鬼神是当时的国家政治大事，须诚心以对。但孔子主张对神鬼适可而止，反对一味祈求神灵保佑而放弃自身努力。这是儒家人本主义思想的体现。

**【句例】**

1. 长期以来我只是把注意力都放在体育锻炼方面，对医生则是敬而远之。

For a long time I have focused only on physical exercise. As to doctors, I *keep aloof from them while showing respect to them*.

2. 他身居高位，傲慢暴躁，所有的下属都对他敬而远之。

In his high position he was arrogant and irritable, so all his subordinates chose to *shun* him.

# 061　举一反三

to draw inferences about three cases from one instance
to ponder a problem by inferences
从一件事情类推而知道其他许多事情
借助推论来思考问题

## 【出处】

子曰："不愤不启，不悱不发。举一隅不以三隅反，则不复也。"（论语 7.8）

The Master said, "Never give (a student) enlightenment unless he has racked his brains and yet fails to understand, or unless he has tried hard to express himself but fails to open his mouth. Never teach him more if he cannot draw inferences about three cases from one instance."

Note: This reveals Confucius' heuristic method in teaching. Confucius meant that only when the learner had a very strong desire to get to know a thing would he begin to explain it to him. And he also required a student to draw inferences about other cases from one instance so that he could deepen his understanding by analogy.

## 【今译】

孔子说："不到学生想弄明白而实在弄不明白的时候，不去开导他；不到他想说而实在说不出来的时候，不去启发他。教给他一个方面的东西，他却不能举一反三，那就不再多教他什么东西了。"

## 【注释】

1. 举一隅不以三隅反：告诉他一个角落里的东西，他就能推知其他三个角落里的东西，即举一反三。隅，角落。

2. 不复：不再教，不多教。

## 【解读】

本句讲孔子以启发式教育充分调动学生学习上的主观能动性。学习者通过自己心理欲望求得的知识，往往更能牢记不忘。此外，学了知识还要能举一反三，应用到更广阔的方面，这样知识就更牢记了。

**【句例】**

1. 我们必须从这次事故举一反三，进一步加强安全教育和管理。

We must *draw inferences about other cases from this* accident, and further strengthen safety education and management.

2.你们思考问题要善于举一反三，才能加深理解，触类旁通。

You have to be good at *pondering a problem by inferences* so that you can deepen your understanding by analogy.

# 062　举直措枉

to promote the upright officials and position them above the crooked
to appoint upright officials and remove the crooked ones
提拔正直无私的官员，置于邪曲的官员之上
任用贤能官员，罢黜奸邪之辈（后世解读）

【出处】

哀公问曰："何为则民服？"孔子对曰："举直错诸枉，则民服；举枉错诸直，则民不服。"（论语2.19）

Prince Ai asked Confucius, "What should be done in order to win obedience from the people?"

The Master replied, "Promote the upright officials and position them above the crooked, then the people will obey.

"If you promote the crooked officials and position them above the upright, the people will not obey."

Note: Confucius put forth a very important principle of governance: putting the upright officials in important positions above the crooked ones.

【今译】

鲁哀公问："怎样才能使百姓服从呢？"孔子回答说："把正直无私的官员提拔起来，置于邪曲的官员之上，老百姓就会服从了；把邪曲的官员提拔起来，置于正直的官员之上，老百姓就不会服从统治了。"

【注释】

1. 举直：把正直的官员提拔起来。举，提拔；直，正直公平的人，此处指正直的官员。

2. 错诸枉：把他们（正直的官员）安置在邪曲的官员之上。错，同"措"，放置；诸，之于；枉，邪曲的人。另一种解读是，任用贤能官员，罢黜奸邪之辈。

【解读】

孔子认为，为政者在任用官员时要选贤任能，以正压邪，才能得到百姓的拥护。

【句例】

1. 如果上面能举直措枉，下面的一些邪曲官员自然会有所收敛。

If the higher authority can *promote the upright officials and position them above the crooked*, those crooked officials will naturally become restrained.

2. 若能举直措枉，那些奸邪官员便不能再乱政了。

If *upright officials are appointed and the crooked ones are removed*, the latter will not be able to disrupt the governance.

# 063　君子不器

A superior man is not a utensil.
A high official does not necessarily have a specific skill.
君子不像器具那样（只有某一方面的用途）。
高级官员不一定要有具体的技能。

**【出处】**

子曰："君子不器。"（论语 2.12）

The Master said, "A superior man is not a utensil."

Note: Confucius pointed out that a high-ranking official should have comprehensive administrative skills rather than have just one specific skill like an everyday utensil that has only one specific usage.

**【今译】**

孔子说："君子不像器具那样（只有某一方面的用途）。"

**【注释】**

1. 君子不器：君子必须掌握治理家国的通盘领导才干而不拘于一才一艺。器，器具，借喻只有具体才艺的人。

**【解读】**

孔子认为，君子（指当时的高级官员）应当博学多识，具有安邦济世的才干，而不应局限于具体的某一技艺，这样才能通观全局、领导全局，成为合格的领导者。

**【句例】**

1. 古人说的君子不器，是指高级官员必须具备统领全局的能力，而不必具备某些具体的技能。

When the ancients said that *a superior man was not a utensil*, they meant that high-ranking officials must have overall management capacity and did not have to own some specific skills.

2. 一个金融机构的执行总裁不会制作 PPT（幻灯片演示文件）其实很正常。君子不器嘛。

It's quite normal that the CEO of a financial institution cannot make a PowerPoint file. *A high-ranking manager does not necessarily have a specific skill, right?*

# 064　君子固穷

A man of virtue maintains steadfast in adversity.
A gentleman should keep moral integrity in a plight.
君子能在困厄中固守道德底线。
君子必须在困境中保持道德操守。

【出处】

在陈绝粮，从者病，莫能兴。子路愠见曰："君子亦有穷乎？"子曰："君子固穷，小人穷斯滥矣。"（论语 15.2）

Running out of food while besieged in Chen, Confucius and his followers became too hungry to rise to their feet.

Zilu was annoyed. He came up to the Master and said, "Must a man of virtue be caught in such adversity?"

"A man of virtue maintains steadfast in adversity, while a base man may act recklessly in it," replied the Master.

Note: When Confucius and his men were on their way to the State of Chu, some people from the State of Chen detained them because they feared that they would go and help the State of Chu and become a threat to them. It was at that time that Confucius required his disciples to maintain their moral integrity even when they were trapped in adversity.

【今译】

孔子一行在陈国断了粮食，随从的人饿坏了，都站立不起来了。子路很不高兴地来见孔子，说道："君子也有困厄的时候吗？"孔子说："君子虽遭困厄，却还能固守（道德底线）；小人一遇困厄就胡作非为了。"

【注释】

1. 固穷：遭遇贫穷和困厄而固守原则不失气节。穷，贫穷，困厄。
2. 穷斯滥：胡作非为不加节制。滥，过多，过分。

【解读】

此句讲孔子带领弟子前往楚国的途中，在陈国和蔡国交界处遭不明真相的兵士的围困。孔子的个别学生想不通，觉得他们一直在为国为民奔波，遭此困厄实在是不公平。但孔子教导他们，要成大事，难免会遭受困厄，关键是在困厄之际要能固守原则，不失气节。

【句例】

1. 君子固穷，任何情况下都不会胡作非为危害社会。

*A man of virtue maintains steadfast in adversity* and will never do harm to society by acting recklessly.

2. 我祖父牢记君子固穷的古训，几十年如一日坚守乡村的教职。

My grandfather kept in mind the ancient motto that *a gentleman should keep moral integrity in a plight* and persisted in his teaching position in the countryside for decades.

# 065  君子坦荡荡

A gentleman is open and broad-hearted.
to be open and poised
君子坦诚而心胸宽广
开朗而泰然自若

**【出处】**

子曰："君子坦荡荡，小人长戚戚。"（论语 7.37）

The Master said, "A gentleman is open and broad-hearted; a base man is always worried and distressed."

Note: According to Confucius, a gentleman, or a virtuous person, is always happy because he is broad-hearted, and he often wears a composed look. A base man is constantly on the alert and lives in fear and worries, and will tend to have a woeful mood and wear a miserable look.

**【今译】**

孔子说："君子坦诚而心胸宽广，小人经常忧虑哀伤。"

**【注释】**

1. 坦荡荡：心胸宽广、开阔、容忍。
2. 长戚戚：经常忧愁、烦恼的样子。

**【解读】**

按孔子的说法，君子总是快乐的，因为他心胸宽广，脸上经常带着一种沉稳的表情。小人总是怕这怕那，生活在恐惧和担忧中，脸上往往会有一种忧愁的表情。

**【句例】**

1. 君子坦荡荡，我对你们没有什么不能说的。

*A gentleman is open and broad-hearted*, so I have nothing to conceal from you.

2. 看一个人是坦荡荡还是长戚戚，最能看出他面对困难时的真实心态。

To see whether he is *open and poised* or worried and distressed is the best way to perceive a person's true mentality in face of difficulty.

# 066　君子之过

the fault of a superior man
the fault of a gentleman
地位高的官员所犯的错误
品行高尚的人所犯的错误

【出处】

子贡曰："君子之过也，如日月之食焉。过也，人皆见之；更也，人皆仰之。"（论语 19.21）

Zigong said, "The faults of a superior man are like the eclipses of the sun and the moon. When he has his faults, all men witness them; when he has mended them, all men look up to him with admiration."

Note: According to Zigong, an excellent disciple of Confucius, when a noble man makes a mistake, others can see it clearly, but as long as he dares to admit his mistake and correct it immediately, his reputation will not be affected and he will still be admired by people.

【今译】

子贡说："君子的过错好比日蚀或月蚀。他犯错误，人们都看得见；他改正错误，人们就更加敬仰他。"

【注释】

1. 仰：仰望，敬仰。

2. 君子之过：指品行高尚的人或高级领导人所犯的错误，其特点是知错能改，改了后更加受人尊重。

【解读】

按子贡的说法，品行高尚的人犯错误，别人看得很清楚，但只要他勇于承认自己的错误，有错必改，就不会影响自己的声誉，仍然会得到人们的景仰。

【句例】

1. 如果一个领导人勇于改正错误，那么他的错误就是君子之过。人民是会原谅他的。

If a leader dares to correct his mistakes. His will be *the faults of a superior man* and the people will pardon him.

2.他勇于承认错误，及时改正错误，大家照样敬仰他。那是君子之过。

He admitted his faults boldly and corrected them in time, and everyone respected him all the same. That was the fault of a gentleman.

# 067  侃侃而谈

to have amiable and fluent talks
to talk with ease and fluency
从容不迫地说话

---

**【出处】**

朝，与下大夫言，侃侃如也；与上大夫言，訚訚如也。（论语 10.2）

The Master had amiable and fluent talks at court with ministers of lower grades. To ministers of upper grades, he spoke rightly and reverently.

Note: This chapter tells how Confucius spoke appropriately and behaved rightly at court.

**【今译】**

孔子在朝堂里同下大夫说话，显得从容不迫、刚直而温和；同上大夫说话，显示得刚直而恭敬。

**【注释】**

1. 侃侃如：说话刚直温和、从容不迫的样子。侃，刚直、和乐。

2. 訚訚如：正直而恭敬的样子。

**【解读】**

此句记孔子在朝廷对待同事和国君谦恭坦诚而温和自然，言行举止合乎礼仪。

**【句例】**

1. 面对那么多听众他侃侃而谈，从但丁的《神曲》谈到尼采的超人哲学。

Facing the large audience he *had amiable and fluent talks*, from Dante's *Divine Comedy* to Nietzsche's superman philosophy.

2. 两小时过去了他还在台上侃侃而谈，却没看到台下已空无一人了。

Two hours passed and he was still on the stage *talking with ease and fluency* without noticing that all the audience had gone.

# 068  克己复礼

to exercise self-restraint and resume
the observation of the rules of propriety
to restrain personal desires and observe the social norms
克制自己，恢复对礼的遵守
克制自己，恢复对社会规范的遵守

---

**【出处】**

颜渊问仁。子曰："克己复礼为仁。一日克己复礼，天下归仁焉。"（论语12.1）

When Yan Yuan asked what benevolence was, the Master said, "To exercise self-restraint and resume the observation of the rules of propriety will mean benevolence. Once everybody has become self-restrained and observed the rules of propriety again, benevolence will prevail in the whole kingdom."

Note: Confucius wrote a prescription for the disordered society: the suppression of personal desires, the observance of the rules of propriety, and the establishment of a society full of benevolence.

**【今译】**

颜渊问什么叫做仁。孔子说："克制自己，一切都照着礼的要求去做，这就是仁。一旦大家都这样做，天下就能回归到仁德盛行的状态了。"

**【注释】**

1. 克己：克制自己，约束自身。
2. 复礼：使思想言行符合礼的要求。

**【解读】**

孔子为当时的乱世开出的药方是：抑制个人欲望，遵守礼法，建立一个充满仁爱的社会。

**【句例】**

1. 孔子提出克己复礼，是为了抑制贪欲和争战，回归理想社会状态。

Confucius put forward the idea of *exercising self-restraint and resuming the observation of the rules of propriety* in order to constrain greed and contending and return to the ideal social state.

2. 在当今社会，我们仍然须要克己复礼。

We still need to *restrain our personal desires and observe the social norms*.

# 069  空空如也

The mind goes blank.
totally empty
脑子一片空白（原意）
什么也没有（今意）

【出处】

子曰："吾有知乎哉？无知也。有鄙夫问于我，空空如也。我叩其两端而竭焉。"（论语 9.8）

The Master said, "Am I knowledgeable? I am not. Once when a countryman sought advice from me about a problem, my mind went blank. Then I analyzed its extremes and managed to have it solved."

Note: When someone asked Confucius a question, he said he first felt that his mind went blank, but then he thought of an analytical method to seek an appropriate solution to a problem, and that is the doctrine of the mean. On this principle, he would rule out all extreme possibilities when solving a problem, and tried to find a best possible solution.

【今译】

孔子说："我有知识吗？其实没有知识。有一个乡下人问我一个问题，我脑子里好像空空的。我于是从问题的正反两面去分析，尽力引导他找出解决办法。"

【注释】

1. 鄙夫：乡下人。

2. 空空如也：指脑子一片白，现在则指一无所有。

3. 叩：问，询问，这里指分析研究。

4. 两端：两头，指正反、始终、上下，这里指事物的两个极端。

5. 竭：穷尽，指尽力究其原因。

## 【解读】

有人问孔子一个问题，孔子说他首先感到自己的大脑一片空白，即空空如也，但后来他想到了一种分析方法来寻求解决问题的适当方法，这就是中庸之道。根据这一原则，他在解决问题时会排除所有极端的可能性，并试图找到一个可能的最佳解决方案。中庸之道是一种避免走极端的、趋利避害的策略运用，用这种方法，往往能得到最适当合理的结果。这是儒家中庸思想的运用。

## 【句例】

1. 股东们要我展望公司的愿景，我脑子空空如也，竟一时语塞。

The shareholders asked me to forecast the company's vision. For the moment *my mind went blank* and could not utter a word.

2. 那年头我只不过是深圳的一个外来工，口袋里总是空空如也，买房纯粹是个梦想。

In those days I was only a migrant laborer in Shenzhen and my pocket used to be *totally empty*. It was a pure dream to buy a house.

# 070　来者可追

What is yet to come can be remedied.
There is still time to amend.
将来的还可以追悔补救
还有时间改正

【出处】

楚狂接舆歌而过孔子曰："凤兮凤兮！何德之衰？往者不可谏，来者犹可追。已而已而！今之从政者殆而！"（论语 18.5）

In the State of Chu, Madman Jieyu passed by Confucius, chanting, "O phoenix! O phoenix! How come you are so unlucky? What has passed cannot be redeemed; what is yet to come can be remedied. Forgo it. Forgo it! Peril awaits those engaged in government today!"

Note: Madman Jieyu (a hermit) tried to persuade Confucius to stop his political pursuits, and live in reclusion to keep his moral integrity in the turbulent days. Confucius liked this man's frankness, but he would not listen to him. Confucius kept doing everything he could hoping that he could save the disordered world, although he knew it was hardly possible for him to succeed.

【今译】

楚国的狂人接舆唱着歌从孔子的车旁走过，他唱道："凤凰啊，凤凰啊，你的德运为何衰微到如此地步？过去的已经无可挽回，未来的还来得及补救。罢了，罢了。如今的执政者危险啊！"

【注释】

1. 楚狂接舆：楚国一个名叫接舆的狂人，隐士。其人已不可考。

2. 往者不可谏，来者犹可追：过去的已无可挽回，将来的还可以补救。追，追悔，补救。

3. 已而：算了吧。接舆劝孔子别再推行他那套治国理念了。

**【解读】**

孔子的一生是跟现实紧密联系着的，他为了社会秩序的恢复和天下的安宁而四处奔波，大声疾呼，希望他的学说能为世所用。相比之下，跟他同时代的不少隐士却坚信社会没救，自己一味消极处世，还反对别人出来救世，接舆就是其中的一个。他把孔子喻为凤鸟，指出他终日奔波而不为时所用，运气不好，不如退隐山林。当然，孔子为救世知其不可为而为之，是不会向他们学习的。

**【句例】**

1. 往者不可谏，来者犹可追。你就好好改造，重新做人吧。

What has passed cannot be redeemed; *what is yet to come can be remedied*. You are well advised to remold yourself to turn over a new leaf.

2. 来者犹可追。你要从跌倒的地方爬起来。

*There is still time to amend*. You have to get up from where you fell.

# 071 老而不死是为贼

At your old age you still wouldn't die. You are a pest!
to be cursed as not to die earlier for being virtueless
老了不去死，真是个祸害。
因无德而被人诅咒早死

**【出处】**

原壤夷俟。子曰："幼而不孙弟，长而无述焉，老而不死，是为贼。"以杖叩其胫。（论语 14.43）

Yuan Rang sat still with his legs stretched apart, waiting for Confucius to approach. Then Confucius came up and said to him, "When young you showed neither modesty nor fraternal love. Having grown up you were good for nothing. Now at your old age you still wouldn't die. You are a pest!"

Note: Yuan Rang was an acquaintance of Confucius. When his mother died and Confucius went and offered his condolence, Yuan didn't stand up to meet him, but sat on the ground like an uncivilized tribesman. Confucius severely criticized him for his impoliteness. He was also disappointed that Yuan had done nothing good for all his life.

**【今译】**

原壤叉开双腿坐着等待孔子的到来。孔子骂他说："年幼的时候，你不谦逊不敬重兄长，长大了又没有什么可说的成就，现在老了却不去死，真是个祸害。"

**【注释】**

1. 原壤：鲁国人，孔子的旧友。
2. 夷俟：岔开双腿而坐。夷，像未开化的少数民族的人一样；俟，等待。
3. 不孙弟：不谦逊、不敬重兄长。孙弟，同"逊悌"。
4. 贼：（动词）戕害，（名词）祸害。

**【解读】**

原壤是孔子的熟人。他母亲去世，孔子前去吊唁时，他没有站起来迎接，而是像一个未开化的部落人一样岔开双脚坐在地上。孔子严厉批评他不礼貌，也对他一辈子一事无成感到失望。

【句例】

1."老而不死是为贼！"这是孔子对一个特定的无德之人的批评。他无意指谪所有的老年人。

"*At your old age you still wouldn't die. You are a pest!*" With this Confucius criticized a particular person who was without virtue. He didn't aim it at old people at large.

2. 人老要积德，不要因为无德而让人骂老而不死。

One should do good to build up virtues when old, lest he should *be cursed as not to die earlier for being virtueless*.

# 072　劳而不怨

to show anxiety rather than discontent
to work hard without making any complaint (a variant)
心里忧虑却没有不满情绪
辛勤劳动而不埋怨（后世用法，非本意）

**【出处】**

子曰："事父母几谏，见志不从，又敬不违，劳而不怨。"（论语 4.18）

The Master said, "In serving your parents, gently remonstrate with them when they are wrong. When seeing that they won't listen to you, respect them all the same rather than offend them, and show your anxiety rather than discontent."

Note: Confucius suggested that a son should express disagreement with his parents in a gentle and tactful way, and try to avoid causing offense or resentment, and when his parents would not listen to him, he could only show anxiety, but should not make any complaint.

**【今译】**

孔子说："服侍父母，劝谏时要委婉。见父母心里不愿听从，仍要恭敬，不要冒犯，心里忧虑却没有不满情绪。"

**【注释】**

1. 几谏：委婉地劝谏。几：隐微，轻发且不过于直白。

2. 违：冒犯。

3. 劳：心忧。《诗经》有"实劳我心""劳心忉忉""劳心忉忉"等句，其中"劳"均为"忧"之意。

**【解读】**

孔子建议儿辈应该以温和和委婉的方式表达与父母的不同意见，并尽量避免引起冒犯或怨恨。当父母不听劝告时，只能表现出焦虑，而不应该抱怨。

【句例】

1. 他苦苦劝阻父亲不要给骗子汇款。面对愤怒的父亲他一直轻声劝说，劳而不怨。

He tried hard to dissuade his father from making a remittance to a cheater. Facing his wrathful father he kept speaking gently, *showing anxiety rather than discontent*.

2. 老百姓知道政府这样做是为了他们的利益，所以大家都服从分工，劳而不怨。

The common people knew that the government was doing so for their interests, so they all obeyed the division of labor, and *worked very hard without making any complaint*.

# 073   乐以忘忧

to forget about one's worries while taking delight in something
to feel happy and unconcerned about the troubles
沉浸在快乐之中而忘掉忧虑

**【出处】**

子曰：“其为人也，发愤忘食，乐以忘忧，不知老之将至云尔。”（论语 7.19）

The Master, "I am no more than a man who forgets his food when racking his brains without a result, who forgets about his worries while taking delight in life, and who cares little about the increasing age."

Note: When someone asked Zilu what Confucius was like, Zilu did not know how to answer, and Confucius told him to make the above reply. That was also the self-evaluation of Confucius. In his later years, Confucius was able to concentrate on teaching and focus on the reformatting of ancient books. Therefore, he was in a happy mood, and was still working hard without knowing that he was getting old.

**【今译】**

孔子说：“他这个人呐，陷于苦思冥想而不得要领之时，连饭都会忘记吃；沉浸在快乐之中而忘掉忧虑，就连自己快老了都不知道，如此而已。”

**【注释】**

1. 发愤：（见 030 注释 2）

**【解读】**

当有人问子路孔子是个怎么样的人时，子路不知该如何回答，孔子就告诉他可以作以上的应答。那也是孔子的自我评价。晚年的孔子一方面专心教学，一方面专注于古籍的整理，能从心所欲，故心情愉快，不顾已经步入了衰老期，依然在忘情地奋斗着。

**【句例】**

1. 山区的孩子有机会读书就是最大的幸运。所以尽管每家都很穷，但同学们读起书来都是乐以忘忧。

Having the chance to go to school was the biggest luck for children in the mountainous areas. So poor as they were, the students all *forgot about their worries while taking delight in* studies.

2. 当时我们的物质生活极端贫乏，但科研工作进展顺利，所以大家都乐以忘忧。

Our material life was extremely poor at that time, but the research work was going well, so everybody was *happy and unconcerned about the troubles* of life.

# 074　乐在其中

That is where one's pleasure lies.
to find pleasure in doing something
乐趣也就在这中间了。
喜欢做某事，并从中获得乐趣

【出处】

子曰："饭疏食饮水，曲肱而枕之，乐亦在其中矣。不义而富且贵，于我如浮云。"（论语 7.16）

The Master said, "Eating coarse food, drinking plain water and lying with my bended arms for a pillow are where my pleasure lies. Riches and ranks acquired by unrighteous means are to me like passing clouds."

Note: Confucius said that he would rather enjoy a simple life than seek fame and riches in an unjust way. And he took pleasure in living a simple life.

【今译】

孔子说："吃粗粮，喝清水，弯着胳膊当枕头，乐趣也就在这中间了。用不正当的手段得来的富贵，对于我来讲就像是天上的浮云一样。"

【注释】

1. 饭疏食：饭，作动词，是"吃"的意思。疏食即粗粮。

2. 曲肱：弯着胳膊。肱，胳膊。

3. 浮云：比喻转瞬即逝、虚而不实的东西。

【解读】

此句孔子讲到了富贵与道的关系问题。他认为只要合乎原则，富贵就可以去追求，否则，他宁愿过着简朴的生活，并以此自得其乐。

【句例】

1. 别人都在玩手机，我侄儿却一直在读书做作业，他说他读书乐在其中，不受环境影响。

While others are immersed in their mobile phones, my nephew has been reading and doing his homework. He says he is not affected by the environment since learning is *where his pleasure lies*.

2. 当一名车工虽然枯燥，他操作起机器来却是乐在其中。

Although it's dull work to be a turner, he still *found pleasure in* operating the machine.

# 075  礼之用和为贵

In carrying out the rules of propriety, harmony is a valued pursuit.
harmony is a valued pursuit (simplified usage)
礼的应用，贵在追求和谐。
和为贵（简化用法）

## 【出处】

有子曰："礼之用，和为贵。"（论语1.12）

Youzi said, "In carrying out the rules of propriety, harmony is a valued pursuit."

Note: The rules of propriety were the topmost code of conduct in Confucius' time. They were used to guide and regulate people's behaviors. People behaved according to such rules so as to guarantee the harmony in society and families. Here Youzi emphasized the restriction function of the rules of propriety and warned that harmony, though a good thing, should not be misused or overused.

## 【今译】

有子说："礼的应用，贵在追求和谐。"

## 【注释】

1. 礼：此处指讲礼的节制功能，它使人们的行为恰到好处，不走极端，从而达到人际关系的和谐。

2. 和：和谐。此处的"和谐"具有"中正、平和、调谐"的深度，而不仅仅停留在人与人之间和睦相处的日常水平。

## 【解读】

孔子时代，礼是最高的行为准则。它被用来指导和规范人们的行为。人们按照这些规则行事，以保证社会和家庭的和谐。

## 【句例】

1. 古代的礼是最高行为准则，其目的之一是节制人的言行使之合乎一定的度，这就是所谓的"礼之用和为贵"。

In ancient times, the rules of propriety were the highest code of conduct, and one of its purposes was to regulate people's words and deeds to a moderate degree. This is what we call "*in carrying out the rules of propriety, harmony is a valued pursuit*".

2. 和为贵。不要再在非原则问题上争执不休了。

*Harmony is a valued pursuit*, so stop arguing over unprincipled issues any longer.

# 076　里仁为美

It is nice to have benevolent neighbors.
It's good to dwell in a benevolence neighborhood where prevails.
居住在仁风盛行的地方才是好的。

## 【出处】

子曰："里仁为美，择不处仁，焉得知？"（论语 4.1）

The Master said, "It is nice to have benevolent neighbors. How can it be wise not to choose to dwell in a neighborhood where benevolence prevails?"

Note: Confucius pointed out that it is good thing to dwell in a neighborhood full of love.

## 【今译】

孔子说："居住在仁风盛行的地方才是好的。如果不选择有仁风的住处，怎能说是明智的呢？"

## 【注释】

1. 里仁：居住在仁风盛行的地方。里，作动词，意为"居住"。
2. 处：居住。
3. 知：同"智"。

## 【解读】

此句孔子讲到了择邻的原则。居于仁风盛行的地方，不但邻里和谐、心境舒畅，而且对自己修身进德很有帮助。孔子把仁风盛行视为邻里之美的要件，对后世选择居住环境的风气有很大的影响。孟母三迁即为一例。

## 【句例】

1. 里仁为美，所以选择在一个有仁风的社区买房子应该是我们的指导原则。

*It is nice to have benevolent neighbors*, so choosing to buy a house in a benevolent neighborhood should be our guiding principle.

2. 如果你认同里仁为美，那么我们这个小区对您来说再合适不过了。

If you agree that *it's good to dwell in a neighborhood where benevolence prevails*, then our neighborhood is a most suitable place for you.

# 077　临深履薄（如临深渊，如履薄冰）

extremely cautious
as if approaching an abyss, or treading on thin ice
极其谨慎，唯恐有失
（谨慎得）好像站在深渊旁边，好像踩在薄冰上面

【出处】

　　曾子有疾，召门弟子曰："启予足！启予手！诗云：'战战兢兢，如临深渊，如履薄冰。'而今而后，吾知免夫，小子！"（论语 8.3）

　　When Zengzi was very ill, he summoned his disciples to the bedside and said, "Uncover my feet! And my hands! The *Book of Poetry* says, 'Be cautious with reverence and awe, as if approaching an abyss, or treading on thin ice.' I know from now on it will save me from any body injury, my boys!"

Note: As he believed that keeping a sound body was the best filial piety to parents, Zengzi had been trying cautiously to avoid any body injure, and now before he died he had his disciples come to confirm that his body was all right so that he could die without any regret.

【今译】

　　曾子有病，把他的学生召集到身边来，说道："掀开被子看看我的脚！看看我的手！《诗》上说：'诚惶诚恐、小心谨慎，好像站在深渊旁边，好像踩在薄冰上面。'从今以后，我知道我的身体是不再会受到毁伤了，弟子们！"

【注释】

　　1. 启：开启，掀开。曾子让弟子们掀开被子看自己的手脚。

　　2. 免：指身体免于毁伤。

【解读】

　　曾子是春秋时有名的大孝子。孔子有"身体发肤受之父母，不敢毁伤"的教导，曾子牢记这点，把不让身体发肤受损作为孝敬父母的重要内容，小心谨慎地保护身体。临终前，他召来弟子到床边，见证自己身体发肤并无受到毁伤，

以证明对得起生养自己的父母，好让自己死而无憾。

【句例】

1. 事关重大，看来我们每个人非得临深履薄不可。

The stakes are high. It seems that we all have to be *extremely cautious*.

2. 三年来我看管您的财物，一刻也没有懈怠，真正是如临深渊，如履薄冰。

For the past three years I have been taking care of your properties without a moment's slack, *as if approaching an abyss, or treading on thin ice*.

# 078 临事而惧

to be alert in face of danger
遇事谨慎戒惧

**【出处】**

子曰："暴虎冯河，死而无悔者，吾不与也。必也临事而惧。好谋而成者也。"（论语 7.11）

"I won't be working with those who would die without any regret in fighting with a tiger barehanded, or crossing a river without a boat," replied the Master. "I certainly need one who is alert in face of danger and resorts to strategy for success."

Note: Zilu was a good disciple of Confucius', but he was often obtrusive and in lack of strategy, so Confucius warned him that he should be cautious in face of danger and good at using strategy for success.

**【今译】**

孔子说："赤手空拳和老虎搏斗，徒步涉水过河，死了都不会后悔的人，我是不会和他共事的。我要共事的，一定要是遇事谨慎戒惧，善于谋划而能完成任务的人。"

**【注释】**

1. 暴虎：空手打虎。

2. 冯河；没有桥或船而渡河。冯，音 píng。

**【解读】**

子路是孔子最重要的弟子之一，他性格爽直，果敢刚烈，为人勇武，信守承诺，忠于职守。但孔子总觉得他的勇武有余而谋略不足，所以从暗示他遇事要小心，危险时刻要有戒惧心，处事要多动脑子。

【句例】

1. 他是个临事而惧、好谋而成的人，可以让他去处理这个危局。

He can be sent to cope with the crisis as he *is alert in face of danger* and good at using strategy for success.

2. 临事而惧不是胆怯，而是一种谨慎的态度。

*To be alert in face of danger* doesn't mean timidity. It reflects a prudent attitude.

# 079　苗而不秀　秀而不实

plants grow without blossoming
plants blossom without bearing fruits
庄稼长了苗而没有开花
庄稼开了花而没有结果

【出处】

子曰："苗而不秀者有矣夫；秀而不实者有矣夫！"（论语 9.22）

The Master said, "There are some plants that grow without blossoming, and there are others that blossom without bearing fruits."

Note: Confucius implied that there might be some people who learned or self-cultivated seriously but did not have a result in the end. According to him, learning and self-cultivating were the first two important requirements for a person to succeed and live a meaningful life, but some people might not achieve their goal even though they tried very hard in these two aspects, and Yan Yuan was believed to be one of them.

【今译】

孔子说："庄稼长了苗而不能吐穗扬花的情况是有的，吐穗扬花而不结果实的情况也有。"

【注释】

1. 秀：开花。这里指庄稼吐穗扬花。

2. 实：结果实。

【解读】

本句孔子以"苗而不秀"和"秀而不实"比喻人有好的资质，却没有成就或不幸夭折，一般认为孔子在这里是在痛惜颜回虽然努力学习刻苦修身却最终没出成果。也可以认为是孔子在指出一种普遍现象，即努力学习刻苦修身的人并不一定都能成才。这种情况古今都有。

**【句例】**

1. 他来不及有所成就便不幸早亡，真是苗而不秀啊。

Unluckily he died young before he could accomplish something. He's really *a plant that grows without blossoming*.

2. 作为一名资深教师，他从他学生的身上见过了太多的苗而不秀和秀而不实。

*Some plants grow without blossoming; others blossom without bearing fruits.* As a senior teacher he has seen more of this phenomenon in his students.

# 080　敏而好学

bright and keen on learning
bright and eager to learn
聪敏勤勉而好学

【出处】

子曰："敏而好学，不耻下问，是以谓之文也。"（论语 5.15）

The Master said, "He was bright and keen on learning; he felt no shame in consulting his inferiors! That's why his posthumous title is WEN."

Note: Before this sentence, Zigong asked his teacher Confucius why Kongwenzi (a minister of the State of Wei) was given the posthumous title "Wen". Confucius explained that Kongwenzi was worthy of the title because he was keen on learning and felt no shame in consulting his inferiors. In ancient China, a king or an important official would be given a title when he died to sum up his merits or demerits, and those two merits of Kongwenzi belonged to the category of "WEN", which was one of the best titles one could get.

【今译】

孔子说："他聪敏勤勉而好学，不以向比他地位卑下的人请教为耻，所以给他谥号叫'文'。"

【注释】

1. 敏：聪敏，勤勉。

2. 文：古代帝王或高级官员死后的谥号。"文"是最好的谥号之一。

【解读】

本句之前，孔子的学生子贡问孔子说：孔文子（卫国大臣）凭什么得到"文"的谥号？孔子解释说孔文子敏而好学、不耻下问。在中国古代，国王或重臣去世时都会被授予一个谥号，以总结他的功过，而孔文子的这两个优点属于"文"的范畴，这是一个人能得到的最好的头衔之一。

【句例】

1. 他自幼敏而好学，长大后师法当时的一位著名书法家，最终成为中国古代最优秀的书法家之一。

In his childhood he was *bright and keen on learning*. When he grew up he learned from a famous calligrapher in his time, and eventually became one of the best calligraphers in ancient China.

2. 奶奶经常谈到我爸爸小时候敏而好学，博闻强识。

Grandma often talked about how my father was *bright and eager to learn* when young, and how he had wide learning and a powerful memory.

# 081   民无信不立

A state cannot stand without public confidence.
Without good faith the people will get no footing. (a variant)
没有民众的信任，国家便无法立足
老百姓不讲诚信将无法立足。（后世变体，非原意）

## 【出处】

子贡问政。子曰："足食，足兵，民信之矣。"子贡曰："必不得已而去，于斯三者何先？"曰："去兵。"子贡曰："必不得已而去，于斯二者何先？"曰："去食。自古皆有死，民无信不立。"（论语12.7）

When Zigong asked about how to govern a state, the Master said, "Let there be sufficient food supplies, sufficient armaments, and the public confidence."

"Suppose one of the three has to be crossed out," asked Zigong, "which do you think must go first?" "The armaments," said the Master.

"Suppose one of the remaining two has to be crossed out, which must go now?" Zigong asked again.

"The food supplies," said the Master, "for death befalls all men alike in all times, but a government cannot stand without public confidence."

Note: Confucius pointed out that a state ruler should ensure that the state has sufficient food supplies and military equipment, but the most important thing is to gain trust from the people, because without the trust and support of the people, the state or government could not stand firm.

## 【今译】

子贡问怎样治国。孔子说，"要有充足的粮食，充足的军备，还要老百姓信任它。"子贡说："如果不得不去掉其中一项，那么三者中先去掉哪一项呢？"孔子说："去掉军备。"子贡说："如果不得不再去掉一项，那么剩下两者中去掉哪一项呢？"孔子说："去掉粮食。自古以来人总是要死的，但若不能赢得百姓的信赖，国家就无法立足。"

【注释】

1. 民无信：如果没有老百姓的信赖。后世说的"如果老百姓不讲信用则无法立足"不符合原文，但仍然可以用。

【解读】

孔子指出为政者要保证国家有充足的粮食和军备，但最重要的是要取信于民，因为没有老百姓的信任和支持，国家或政府就无法立足。

【句例】

1. 民无信不立，所以国家和政府一定不能失信于民。

*A state cannot stand without public confidence.* Thus a country and its government must not lose the trust of the people.

2. 孔子说过"民无信不立"。有人误为"老百姓不讲诚信便无法立足"。

Confucius once said "*A state cannot stand without public confidence.*" Some mistake it as "*Without good faith the people will get no footing.*"

# 082 名正言顺 名不正言不顺

If a statement is made in a licit name, it will be justifiable.
justifiable
It won't be justifiable without a licit name.
unjustifiable
名分正，说话就合理顺当。
正当有理的
名分不正，（说话或做事）就不合理法。
（说话或做事）无正当理由的

**【出处】**

子曰："名不正则言不顺，言不顺则事不成。"（论语 13.3）

The Master said, "If a statement is not made in a licit name, it will not be justifiable. If the statement is not justifiable, the goal will not be achieved."

Note: Confucius pointed out that a licit name was a must in order to justify a conduct or the person who conducts.

**【今译】**

孔子说："名分不正，说起话来就不合理顺当，说话不合理顺当，事情就办不成。"

**【注释】**

1. 名：名分。古人说的话和做的事，凡重要者，都要符合自己的身份，要用合理的名义。

**【解读】**

本句之前，孔子和弟子子贡讨论卫灵公死后他孙子和儿子争权的问题。子贡认为卫灵公的儿子搞内乱被放逐，由孙子继位正当合理，他儿子回来争位是不对的。孔子则认为卫灵公的孙子要继位，首先要正名分。暗示做儿子的不能与父亲争位，否则便是不孝，便是名不正而言不顺。"名不正则言不顺，名不顺则事不成"这个名言直到今天还非常重要，一般指一个重要言论的宣示或一件大事的实施，须有正当的名义为支撑，否则就不合理法。

【句例】

1. 总经理发动公司员工为地震灾区捐款是名正言顺的。

It is *justifiable* for the general manager to mobilize the employees to donate money for the earthquake-stricken areas.

2. 你这个通知名不正言不顺。

Your announcement is *unjustifiable* (not made in a licit name).

# 083    鸣鼓而攻之

to beat the drum and launch an attack
to issue a joint condemnation
敲响战鼓，发动进攻
一致声讨

【出处】

季氏富于周公，而求也为之聚敛而附益之。子曰："非吾徒也。小子鸣鼓而攻之可也。"（论语 11.17）

The Jisun Family was wealthier than some lords of the Kingdom of Zhou, and yet Ran Qiu further added to its wealth by all sorts of villainous means. Speaking of Ran Qiu, the Master said, "He is no disciple of mine. You pupils may beat the drum to launch an attack against him."

Note: Confucius expressed his indignation over his disciple Ran Qiu who managed to help make the royal Jisun Family even wealthier by increasing tax burdens on the common people.

【今译】

季氏比周室的公卿还要富有，而冉求还帮他搜刮来增加他的钱财。孔子说："他不再是我的学生了，你们可以大张旗鼓地去声讨他！"

【注释】

1. 聚敛：用不正当手段积聚和收集钱财，即搜刮。

2. 附益：增加。

3. 鸣鼓而攻之：古时打仗用语，击鼓以示进攻，鸣金以示收兵。这里比喻宣布某人罪状加以大力声讨鞭挞。

【解读】

本句讲孔子因高徒冉有为季氏积聚财富而对他提出激烈的批评。冉有又称冉求，他多才多艺，有军事才能，尤擅长理财。当时冉有正担任季氏宰臣，想利用改变田赋制度增加赋税，为季氏聚敛财富。冉有为此事征求孔子意见，孔子明确告诉他要"敛从其薄"，但他没有听老师的话，所以孔子才会那么愤怒。不过，冉有对孔子的事业一贯很支持。后来在孔子的教导下，他逐渐向仁德靠拢，其性情也因此而逐渐完善。

【句例】

1. 如果我说这计划缺陷太大不能用，你们必定会对我鸣鼓而攻之。

If I say this plan is too flawed to work, you people will certainly *beat the drum and launch an attack against* me.

2. 我仅仅说了句那部电影不是那么好，结果全体室友一致对我鸣鼓而攻之。

I was subject to my roommates' *joint condemnation* simply because I said the movie was not so good.

# 084 默而识之

to learn by heart and bear in mind what is learned
默记所学知识

## 【出处】

子曰："默而识之，学而不厌，诲人不倦，何有于我哉？"（论语 7.2）

The Master said, "Learning by heart and bearing in mind what is learned, studying without satiety and teaching without weariness—what difficulty is there for me to do so?"

Note: Learning by heart and bearing in mind what is learned was an important studying method that Confucius introduced.

## 【今译】

孔子说："默记所学知识，学习从不满足，教书育人不知疲倦，这些对我来说有什么难呢？"

## 【注释】

1. 识：同"志"，"记住"的意思。
2. 何有：何难之有。有什么难呢？

## 【解读】

本句的"默而识之"是孔子提出的一个重要学习方法，它强调知识记忆的必要性。

## 【句例】

1. 默而识之的学习方法尽管显得有点古板，但在今天也不能说完全没用。

As a learning method, *learning by heart and bearing in mind what is learned* may seem a bit conservative, but it can't be regard as useless today.

2. 知识记忆的必要性毋庸置疑。默而识之是其重要方法之一。

The necessity of memorizing knowledge cannot be questioned. And *learning by heart and bearing in mind what is learned* is one important method.

# 085　谋道不谋食

（A superior man）seeks for the Way rather than food.
to seek for the truth rather than food
（君子）考虑的是求道而不是衣食问题。
求道而不求食

【出处】

子曰："君子谋道不谋食。耕也，馁在其中矣；学也，禄在其中矣。君子忧道不忧贫。"（论语 15.32）

The Master said, "A superior man seeks for the Way rather than food. Farming might mean hunger while learning might mean salary. A superior man concerns himself with the Way rather than worry about poverty."

Note: In Confucius' time, educational resources were still quite scarce, so Confucius thought that the aim of education should be to provide virtuous and talented educated people to help with governance. According to him, those few who had the opportunity to receive education should be given official posts to help serve the state. And they should all aim high and concern themselves with the Way. The Way here refers to great issues like the principles, the policies and methods of state administration, and earning bread should not become their main task.

【今译】

孔子说："君子考虑的是求道与行道，而不考虑衣食问题。耕田，常常要饿肚子；读书，可以得到俸禄。君子只担心能否求道行道，不担心贫穷。"

【注释】

1. 谋道不谋食：要考虑"道"，而不要把注意力放在谋生上。"道"在这里指有关修身、齐家、治国、平天下的大原则问题。

2. 馁：（něi）饥饿。

【解读】

孔子时代，教育资源仍然相当匮乏，因此孔子认为教育的目的应该是提供贤能的受教育者来帮助治理国家。按他的说法，那些少数有机会接受教育的人应该获得官位，以便为国家服务，故应志存高远。这里的"道"指的是国家管理的原则、政策和方法等重大问题，挣钱谋生不应该成为他们的主要任务。

**【句例】**

1. 君子谋道不谋食。你要多关心国家大事，不要成天为五斗米而操心。

*A superior man seeks for the Way rather than food.* You should pay more heed to the state affairs, and don't be always worried about your bread.

2. 年轻时我父亲常常埋怨我不事农耕。我说我是君子，谋道不谋食。

When I was young, my father used to complain that I didn't do farm work. I said I was a man of lofty idea, and I *sought for the truth rather than food.*

# 086  没齿无怨

never lodge any complaint for all one's life
never complain
至死都不抱怨
从不抱怨

## 【出处】

或问管仲。曰："人也。夺伯氏骈邑三百，饭疏食，没齿无怨言。"（论语 14.9）

When someone asked about Guan Zhong, the Master said, "That's a man of talents. He deprived the Bo Family of the Town of Pian, which was their feudality with three hundred households, only to make them live off coarse food, yet for all their lives the Bo Family never lodged any complaint. "

Note: Guan Zhong was highly appreciated by Confucius. He was the most important prime minister of the State of Qi and is even famous today for his reform which helped make Qi a powerful state at that time. The chief of the Bo Family had committed crimes so Guan Zhong deprived them of the Town of Pian according to the law he made. This showed how correct Guan was in handling the problems concerning the royal families without begetting their resentment or causing any trouble. That was why Confucius said he was a man of great talents.

## 【今译】

有人问管仲是怎样的人。孔子说："他是个有才干的人，他把伯氏骈邑的三百家夺走，使伯氏吃粗茶淡饭，直到老死也没有怨言。"

## 【注释】

1. 人：这里指人才。
2. 伯氏：齐国的大夫。
3. 骈邑：地名，伯氏的采邑。
4. 没齿不怨：到死都不抱怨，从不抱怨。没齿，死的委婉说法。

【解读】

此句是孔子对齐国卿相管仲的较高评价。管仲不但通过变法使齐国强盛，助齐桓公称霸，而且平时执法公允，效果好，孔子认为他是个人才。史载伯氏有罪，管仲为相，奉齐桓公之命依法剥夺了伯氏的采邑三百户。管仲处事得当，让伯氏口服心服，始终无怨言。

【句例】

1. 虽然妻子对我管得太严，但都是为了我好。我对她没齿不怨。

Although my wife was too strict with me, it was all for my good. I never *lodged any complaint* against her *for all my life*.

2. 那段艰难岁月锻炼了我，我对它没齿不怨。

That hard time tempered me, and I *never complained* about it.

# 087 内省不疚

to find nothing to reproach on one's conscience after introspection
to feel no guilt after self-examination
通过反省发现自己问心无愧
自我反省后没有负罪感

## 【出处】

子曰："内省不疚，夫何忧何惧？"（论语 12.4）

The Master said, "When you find nothing to reproach on your conscience after introspection, what is there to be anxious about and what is there to fear?"

Note: Confucius' disciple Sima Niu was worried about the fact that his brother Huantui rebelled against the ruler of the State of Song. Now Confucius told him not to worry about it since it was not his fault.

## 【今译】

孔子说："自己问心无愧，那还有什么忧愁和恐惧呢？"

## 【注释】

1. 内省：内心的自我反省。
2. 疚：愧疚。

## 【解读】

孔子弟子司马牛因其兄桓魋犯上作乱而忧虑，孔子用"内省不疚"来劝他不要忧愁和恐惧，因为犯罪出逃的是他哥哥，那不是他的错，而他也从宋国逃到了鲁国，已经没有危险了。

## 【句例】

1. 尽管那么多人一直在攻击我，但我内省不疚。

Although so many people have been attacking me, I *find nothing to reproach on my conscience after introspection*.

2. 董事长说在这个问题上他内省不疚，不会道歉。

The chairman of the board said he *felt no guilt* on this matter *after self-examination* and would not apologize.

# 088　能近取譬

to put oneself in other people's place
to put oneself in other people's shoes
能推己及人
替别人着想

**【出处】**

子曰："夫仁者，己欲立而立人，己欲达而达人。能近取譬，可谓仁之方也已。"（论语 6.30）

The Master said, "Such is a perfectly virtuous man: while he strives to gain his footing in society, he helps others to gain theirs; while he strives to make his own accomplishment, he helps others to make theirs. And in doing so, he puts himself in other people's place. Such is the way to moral perfection."

Note: Confucius pointed out that a man of perfect virtue should be considerate of others and not impose his own will on others. This is the philosophy of reciprocity which has helped make Confucius one of the greatest social philosophers in the world.

**【今译】**

孔子说："所谓仁人，就是自己想要立足社会，也要帮助他人立足社会；自己想要成功，也要帮助他人成功。凡事能设身处地为他人着想，可以说就是实行仁的方法了。"

**【注释】**

1. 能近取譬：能够就自身打比方，设身处地为他人着想。

**【解读】**

孔子之道，以忠恕二字贯穿其中。立己立人，达己达人，讲的正是忠，就是尽心为人。能近取譬，讲的是恕。恕就是推己及人、为他人着想、不把自己的意志强加给别人，也就是他提出的己所不欲勿施于人的恕道。孔子在上一句讲忠，下一句讲恕，把忠恕之道都向学生交待清楚，并告诉学生这是达到仁的高度的方法。

【句例】

1. 他一向能近取譬，故从教几十年来他真正做到了桃李无言，下自成蹊。

He always *placed himself in other people's place*, so after tens of years he remained a good teacher of fewer words with plenty of followers.

2. 做到能近取譬，你就不会强加于人。

When you *put yourself in other people's shoes*, you will not impose anything on them.

# 089  讷言敏行

slow in speech and prompt in action
cautious in speech and prompt in action
说话慢，行动快
说话要谨慎，行动要敏捷

**【出处】**

子曰："君子欲讷于言而敏于行。"（论语 4.24）

The Master said, "A superior man should be slow in speech and prompt in action."

Note: Confucius pointed out that one should be cautious in speech and active in action.

**【今译】**

孔子说："君子说话要谨慎，但行动要敏捷。"

**【注释】**

1. 讷：说话迟钝、慢，比喻说话谨严，想好了才说。

2. 敏：敏捷，快速。

**【解读】**

此句孔子告诫人们不要出言太快，也就是说要先经过思考后才开口，说出来的话要抓紧落实。早期儒家最看重的修养之一就是慎言敏行。

**【句例】**

1. 告诉人力资源部，此人讷言敏行，就让他在财务部当会计吧。

Tell the HR department that this person is *slow in speech and prompt in action*. Let him be an accountant in the finance department

2. 全体管理人员都必须讷言敏行，这样才能提高本公司的声誉和效能。

The administrative staff should be *cautious in speech and prompt in action*. Only in this way can we improve the reputation and efficiency of our company.

# 090　披发左衽

to wear hair unbound with barbarian clothes on
to be dressed like a barbarian
to be assimilated by outlying tribes
披头散发，衣襟向左开
像未开化的人那样穿着
被外族同化

【出处】

子曰："微管仲，吾其被发左衽矣。岂若匹夫匹妇之为谅也，白经于沟渎而莫之知也。……"（论语 14.17）

The Master said, "But for Guan Zhong, we might now be wearing our hair unbound with barbarian clothes on."

Note: Confucius highly appreciated Guan Zhong for his helping to resist the invasions of the northern uncivilized tribes and his great contributions to the State of Qi and the entire Kingdom of Zhou. Confucius believed that Guan Zhong's efforts helped to avoid the Central Plains being assimilated by the outlying tribes.

【今译】

孔子说："如果没有管仲，恐怕我们也要披散着头发，衣襟向左开了。"

【注释】

1. 微管仲：假如没有管仲。微，无，没有。管仲原为公子纠家臣。公子纠与公子小白（齐桓公）争位被杀，管仲没有自杀殉主，反而应邀担任齐桓公的卿相，助他称霸诸侯，协助他安定天下 40 年。

2. 被发左衽：被，同"披"。衽，衣襟。被发左衽是当时的夷狄之俗，即散发不作髻，上衣瓣襟向左掩，比喻被周边异族同化。

【解读】

桓公任命相管仲，从此开始了富国强兵的争霸历程。管仲说服桓公采用

"尊王攘夷"的政策，以周天子号令天下，扭转了当时诸侯国相互争战杀伐的局面，又积极组织抗击入侵的少数民族，给中原地区带来和平。孔子认为要不是这样，中原地区早已被周边少数民族入侵并同化了，所以他称得上仁。

【句例】

1. 你说我这打扮太正规？你不会要我披发左衽吧？

You mean I dress too formally? You won't expect me to *be dressed like a barbarian*?

2. 要不是我们的老祖宗抗击外族的入侵，我们的民族早在两千多年前就被迫披发左衽了吧。

If our forefathers had not fought against the invasion of outlying tribes more than two thousand years ago, our nation would have been forced to *be assimilated by outlying tribes.*